THE FAMOUS FIVE AND THE MYSTERY OF THE EMERALDS

THE FAMOUS FIVE are Julian, Dick, George (Georgina by rights), Anne and Timmy the dog.

A summer holiday camping on Kirrin Island is the prospect in store for the Five, and they're eagerly looking forward to exploring the island.

But when George overhears a couple of crooks planning a jewel robbery, the Famous Five set off on a dangerous and thrilling trail.

Cover illustration by John Cooper

The Famous Five and the Mystery of the Emeralds

A new adventure of the characters created by Enid Blyton, told by Claude Voilier, translated by Anthea Bell

Illustrated by John Cooper

KNIGHT BOOKS
Hodder and Stoughton

Copyright © Librairie Hachette 1971
First published in France as *Les Cinq Sont Les Plus Fort*

English language translation copyright © Hodder
and Stoughton Ltd. 1981

Illustrations copyright © Hodder and
Stoughton Ltd. 1981

First published in Great Britain by
Knight Books 1981
Seventh impression 1983

British Library C.I.P.

Voilier, Claude
 The famous five and the mystery of the emeralds
 I. Title
843' .91J

 ISBN 0-340-26524-8

Printed and bound in Great Britain for
Hodder and Stoughton Paperbacks, a
division of Hodder and Stoughton Ltd.,
Mill Road, Dunton Green, Sevenoaks,
Kent (Editorial Office: 47 Bedford
Square, London, WC1 3DP) by
Hunt Barnard Printing Ltd.,
Ayelsbury, Bucks.

CONTENTS

Chapter One

OFF FOR THE HOLIDAYS

'This way, Dick! Do hurry up, Anne! I can see an empty compartment! Julian, you hop in first and catch hold of the suitcases!'

George and her cousins, Julian, Dick and Anne, were waiting on the station platform, getting ready to board their train. Julian, the eldest of the children, began to laugh.

'Yes, Master George, *sir*!' he told his cousin, giving her a mock-military salute before he hauled up the little party's suitcases.

As usual, George was jumping up and down with impatience. She looked just like a boy, with her dark hair cut so short, and the determined expression on her brown face. She was eleven, a year younger than Julian. Dick was the same age as George, but unlike her cousin, George could be headstrong and moody – she was always either bubbling over with high spirits, or scowling in one of her bad tempers. She often treated gentle little Anne like a baby. Anne was ten, so she was the youngest of the four cousins.

The children got into the train, and the boys set to work putting the cases up on the luggage rack of the empty compartment George had spotted.

'Phew!' she exclaimed, dropping into her seat. 'The train will be leaving any moment now. What luck to be going off for the holidays again – all four of us together!'

'Yes, and what luck your parents said we three could come and spend the summer with you,' added Julian.

'I do love staying with you at Kirrin, George,' sighed Anne happily. 'Kirrin Cottage is so nice!'

'What *I* like best is being so near the sea,' said Dick. 'There's never a dull moment!'

George jumped to her feet and leaned out of the window.

'Oh, good, we're off! We'll be there in less than two hours' time now. I just can't wait to see Timmy again! I know we all decided he'd really be happier at home, where he can run around as much as he likes, but I've missed him so badly this term!'

Her cousins burst out laughing.

'You feel quite lost without dear old Timothy, don't you?' joked Dick.

'You're right!' George admitted cheerfully.

'Timmy's like a part of me.'

'And he's part of us, too,' said Dick. 'I mean, we wouldn't be able to call ourselves the Five without him, would we? And if you ask me, good old Timmy's as bright as any of us, and certainly he's quick off the mark!'

'Yes, think how he's helped us solve so many of the exciting mysteries that seem to come our way!' said Julian. 'I'm really very fond of your dog, George. I miss him a lot myself!'

The train gathered speed. George, who just couldn't keep still, trod on her cousins' toes as she paced up and down the compartment, and without meaning to she ruffled Anne's hair when her elbow brushed past it.

'Oh, do keep still!' Julian begged her. 'Talk about a live wire! For goodness' sake, calm down!'

George didn't like Julian telling her off, but she sat down again, scowling, and stuck her hands in her pockets just like a boy.

'Dear, dear! Our little Georgina's sulking!' Dick teased her.

Georgina was George's real name, but she simply hated anyone calling her by it. She jumped up again, raising her hand to slap her cousin's face. Laughing, Dick pretended to duck the blow.

'Oh no!' Julian grumbled. 'You're not going to start quarrelling, are you, you two?'

George went back to her corner seat by the doorway and dug her hands into her pockets again. Suddenly, she felt a piece of paper inside one of them. She took it out. It was an envelope!

'Oh, blow!' she muttered. 'I forgot all about this letter! It came yesterday, but I was so busy packing, getting ready for the holidays, I quite forgot to read it. It's from Mother – I expect it's only to tell us to mind we don't miss our train. She's always worrying we'll do that!'

'In that case, it's a bit late to read it,' said Anne, laughing. 'But tell us what it says all the same, George.'

George took the letter out of the envelope and unfolded it. She glanced through it. 'Oh dear!' she exclaimed. 'If only I'd known ... Goodness me, guess what's happened!'

Looking at her audience, who were all listening hard, George dropped her bombshell. 'Mother and Father can't have us at Kirrin Cottage this summer after all!'

Three exclamations of dismay answered her:

'Oh no! But we *must* go!'

'We're already on our way!'

'What shall we do?'

'Apparently there was a dreadful storm at Kirrin last Saturday,' George explained. 'Part of the roof of Kirrin Cottage blew off, and a chimney was smashed – well, the long and short of it is that the house is full of workmen, and there just isn't anywhere for us to sleep. Mother and Father are living in the only rooms that aren't full of builders at work on the repairs. We shall have to go and stay somewhere else.'

'But where?' Julian began.

George didn't reply. Running to the window, she leaned right out, in danger, almost of falling on the railway line.

'Kirrin! It's Kirrin! I *thought* I smelt the sea! We're here! There's the station – and I can see Mother. Oh, she hasn't brought Timmy!'

The train stopped. George left her cousins to get the suitcases out of their compartment. She jumped down on the platform, flung her arms round her mother's neck and gave her a big hug.

'Oh, Mother, it's so nice to see you! How's Father? Why didn't he come too? Did you leave him at home in his kennel?'

She was so excited that she was getting her father and Timmy the dog all mixed up. Aunt Fanny began to laugh.

'Let me go, darling, do – you'll strangle me! Your father's very well. Of course he's wrapped up in his scientific work, as usual. As for Timmy, I'd really rather you didn't meet again for the first time in public. Your reunions are a bit too spectacular for my liking!'

Julian, Dick and Anne hauled their luggage out of the train and gathered round their aunt.

'Hullo, Aunt Fanny!'

'Hullo, children! Good gracious, just look at

the gloomy expressions on your faces! What on earth is the matter?'

'George says you can't have us to stay at Kirrin Cottage this summer after all,' Julian told her. 'So you see, we're rather worried.'

'Well, there's nothing to worry about. Your holidays won't be spoilt, so cheer up! The car's outside, and I'll tell you all about it as we drive along.'

The little party left the railway station. The four cousins piled into the car, and Aunt Fanny took the steering wheel.

'Since there isn't room for you all to sleep in the cottage this summer,' she said as the car started off, 'I suggest you go and camp on Kirrin Island. As you know, the island belongs to George, and I know you've often been over there for the day, and sometimes you've spent the whole night there. Well, this time you can put up tents and live on the island right through the holidays. You can pretend you're Robinson Crusoes!'

The children shouted for joy.

'Oh, hurray! We'll soon feel at home there!'

'Yes, I'm sure we can trust you to look after yourselves,' said Aunt Fanny. 'And if necessary, Uncle Quentin and I won't be far off, so there's nothing to worry about.'

'We have my boat, and our bicycles,' said George. 'And we can buy our provisions in the village.'

'Yes, and camping in the open is very healthy. It will do you good,' said Aunt Fanny. 'Well, first stop Kirrin Cottage, and here we are! Everyone get out!'

The children could see builders at work up on the roof of the cottage. Uncle Quentin came down the garden path to meet the new arrivals.

Suddenly, an enormous, brown, hairy object, moving like lightning, bounded up, making straight for George like an arrow. In a moment, a thick, warm tongue was licking her face all over.

'Timmy – dear old Timmy! Oh, I'm so glad to see you again. I bet you've missed me!'

'Woof!' replied the big dog, wagging his tail.

Then he welcomed the other children too, before trotting ahead of them to the house with his tail held high.

Chapter Two

GEORGE OVERHEARS A PLOT

Early that afternoon, after a good big lunch to keep their strength up, the four children started moving their camping equipment over to Kirrin Island. Of course they took Timmy with them too! The Famous Five wouldn't have been complete without him, and Aunt Fanny and Uncle Quentin were glad to think George and her cousins would have Timmy to guard them. Of course, it was very quiet out here in the country, by the seaside, but you never knew what might happen.

The Five piled into George's stout little rowing boat. Timmy guarded the kit-bags full of the provisions they were taking. Julian and Dick took the oars and rowed, and George held the tiller to steer the boat. Anne was quite happy just admiring the sea and the flight of the gulls swooping through the air, uttering their hoarse cries.

Kirrin Island lay right opposite Uncle Quentin and Aunt Fanny's house, not far out at the entrance to Kirrin Bay. The children had left their bicycles in the little hut which Uncle Quentin had recently had put up at the bottom of the garden of Kirrin Cottage. They made sure the tyres were carefully pumped up so they would be ready to ride. Altogether, the cousins thought the holidays were starting even better than they had expected!

Soon the Five reached Kirrin Island and came on shore. They began by going all over the island, to get to know it again. And it was a lovely place to visit. There were rabbits scurrying through the grass, and jackdaws flying round one of the towers of the ruined castle which stood in the middle of the island.

'How lucky you are to have an island like this, all of your own!' sighed Anne.

'Yes, I am,' George agreed. 'It was awfully generous of my parents to give me Kirrin Island as a present. But don't forget, I said you three could share it with me, so it's yours too!'

The children went through the huge old archway which was the castle entrance, crossed the big courtyard with its cracked paving stones, and ended up in one of the bigger rooms on the ground floor.

'Part of the roof is still all right here, and the walls are standing,' explained George, 'so if the

Kirren Island lay right opposite Uncle Quentin and Aunt Fanny's house.

'I'd rather sleep outside in our tents,' said Anne.

weather is bad we can always take shelter in this room.'

'I'd rather sleep outside in our tents, though,' said Anne. 'I'm a little frightened to be in the castle at night, when the wind goes whistling round the towers.'

'You're just a coward!' Dick told his sister. '*I* think the castle is a wonderful place. One day we must explore the dungeons again – what do you think, George?'

'That sounds a super idea! But now we'd better put the tents up. Come on, everyone, let's get down to work!'

The four cousins soon had their camp ready. They stored their provisions in a sheltered corner of the castle, and made a fireplace for a camp fire in the courtyard. They pitched their tents in the shelter of a wall, which would protect them from any bad weather.

The Five slept well that night. The children dreamed of having adventures, and Tim dreamed of rabbits which just sat there waiting for him to catch them!

Next morning Dick went to fetch water from the spring they had found on the island, and Anne made everyone a delicious breakfast of bacon and eggs and fried bread.

They spent their first day on Kirrin Island out of doors, enjoying themselves exploring. It was fine weather. The sun shone in a cloudless sky, and the sea was so blue that the Five went in to bathe several times.

Next day the children rowed across to the mainland early in the afternoon to say hullo to George's mother and father. Then they got their bicycles out and rode to Kirrin village to stock up with fresh fruit. They thought they had never enjoyed the holidays so much before!

When they were back on the island again, George, who could never keep still for long, suggested a game of hide-and-seek – a new sort of hide-and-seek. 'I'll be the only one to hide,' she explained to her cousins, 'and all three of you must look for me. I bet you don't find me! But you'll have to tie Timmy up to a tree with his lead, or he'll pick up my scent and take you straight to me. All right, I'm off! Close your eyes, count up to fifty – and then try to guess where I am!'

With these words she set off at a run. She was pleased with the idea of the trick she was going to play on her cousins. She had discovered a wonderful hiding place that very morning, and she was sure no one would be able to track her down there.

Still running, she reached the top of the cliff towering above the sea behind the castle.

George was absolutely fearless, and she started to climb down the steep slope of the cliff-face. She clung on with her hands and feet, and did not feel in the least giddy. When she was halfway down the cliff, she stopped and squeezed herself into a little hollowed-out ledge in the rock. She was completely invisible there! No one could see her, either from the top of the cliff or the beach down below. A moment later, she heard Julian looking for her up above.

'I bet she's somewhere here,' he was saying.

'That's what *you* think!' replied Dick. 'The ground's as flat as a pancake just here, so unless she's gone down a rabbit hole . . . '

Her cousins' voices died away. George guessed they were going off to look for her somewhere else. She laughed quietly to herself.

The sea sparkled as it stretched out before her eyes. Then, suddenly, she saw a black spot moving towards the island.

'Hullo – a boat!' she thought. 'I wonder who can be coming here?'

The boat came closer. There were two men on board. George could only see the back view of the man who was rowing. He looked thin, and he had a lot of red hair. The other man, who was facing her, was thick-set, with a big, rather square head. The red-haired man seemed to know how to avoid the dangerous rocks which surrounded the island, and soon the boat came to shore. Its hull scraped on the little beach down below.

'Oh, bother them!' thought George. 'What do they think they're doing on my island? Everyone around here knows that Kirrin Island is private property!'

From where she was hiding she could not see the newcomers any more, but she realised they were getting out of the boat.

Almost immediately, the sound of their voices rose to her. One of the men had a slight foreign accent.

'Good work, Lenny,' he said. 'This was just the place to pick. We needn't worry about anyone overhearing us here, so we can talk quite openly.'

'That's right – the island is uninhabited,' agreed the other voice. 'Apparently the owners hardly ever come here, so that makes it an ideal spot for us to discuss our business in peace and quiet!'

George was just going to call out that she was there – she was a well-brought-up girl, with good manners, and she knew it was not right to eavesdrop on other people's private conversations. But what she heard next at once made her speechless. Instead of warning the men she was up above them, she listened hard, feeling very alarmed.

'And we needed a suitable place to talk,' went on the first voice. 'Somewhere really private – since we're up to no good, as you might say!'

'Up to no good? It all depends which side you're on, Mr Karl!' said the voice of the man called Lenny, as if it were a good joke. 'It won't be very good for our victim, that's for sure – but it'll be good for us all right! Ha, ha, ha!'

'This is no time to be funny!' said the other man, Karl. 'Whichever way you look at it, this is a really big job we're hoping to bring off, so it's high time we planned the details. After all, it's July already, and we must act on July 30th precisely.'

'Yes, and we want to make sure nothing can possibly go wrong. We must have it all thought out in advance. Our success will depend on careful planning.'

George kept absolutely quiet up in her hiding place. She was listening intently. She realised that the two men below her must be planning to commit some sort of crime. If the wind continued blowing towards her and the two strangers did not move farther along the beach, then she had a good chance of hearing the details of their plot.

'I don't see too many risks in the job myself,' said Karl's harsh voice. 'That is, if the information you've given me is correct.'

'I've checked everything, Mr Karl, sir. Don't worry. The house is very isolated, and it stands in a lonely part of the country. There's no need to worry about anyone coming along to disturb us, even in the holiday season – I'm sure of that! Those parts are never very crowded.'

'What I don't like, Lenny, is having to wait till the end of the month before we can act.'

'There's nothing else we can do, Mr Karl. Dave won't be here, in a position to help us, until July 30th. Thanks to him, everything should go off quite smoothly, with as little risk as possible.'

'Yes, I can see that Dave will come in very useful,' agreed Karl. 'Well, I suppose we shall just have to wait patiently.'

*   *   *

Meanwhile, of course, Julian, Dick and Anne were still looking for George on the opposite side of the island.

'This is simply incredible!' said Dick. 'We've been searching everywhere, for over twenty minutes, and there's still no sign of her!'

'If you ask me,' said Anne, in a frightened voice, 'she's made her way down into the castle dungeons, and she's hiding inside one of them. Well, *I'm* certainly not going down to fetch her out!'

'Down into the dungeons? I shouldn't think so!' said Julian, shaking his head. 'I should say it's more likely she's hiding outside the castle, some-where on the other side of the island. I thought it sounded as if she was going that way when she ran off!'

'You think what you like!' said Dick. 'But I'm carrying on exploring this part of the island. Going to help me, Anne?'

'Yes, of course, Dick.'

'Right, I'll help you search this side of the island for another ten minutes,' decided Julian.

'But after that I'm going back to search the other side, where the cliffs are.'

And Julian, Dick and Anne went on searching.

While they were hunting for George in vain, what do you think Timmy was doing? Tied up to a tree beside George's tent, the dog was sniffing the air. Clever old Tim knew exactly where his little mistress was! If he had been free, he would have been trying to scrabble down the cliff-face to her in no time at all!

Suddenly he uttered a faint whine, and his moist black nose twitched. He was feeling afraid. Somehow he knew that George was in danger!

And George was certainly in a very awkward position. She realised that by now she knew far too much about the criminals for her own good. If she was unlucky enough to be discovered here, they were very likely to harm her in some way to keep her quiet.

'Well, after all, they can't see me up here,' the brave girl told herself. 'But this hiding place of mine is so small I'm beginning to get pins and needles. And if I stretch, I might send a pebble rolling down the cliff. If they were to hear me . . .'

As carefully as she possibly could, she tensed and relaxed all her muscles, still listening hard. But the wind had changed, and the men's voices did not float up to her nearly so clearly now.

She heard Lenny say something which she was almost sure was 'the lady of the manor house'.

Then she caught the words, 'Seeing she lives alone, it'll be easy.'

'She must be crazy!' replied Karl. 'It will serve her right! Imagine keeping a jewel case full of precious stones in the house! No one even knows just how much they're worth.'

' ... superb piece of jewellery ... magnificent emeralds ... '

'A family heirloom, isn't it?'

'Yes ... Queen Victoria gave the emeralds to one of her ancestors ... '

'... such a risk ... keeping a treasure like that at home! She must feel sure it's safe enough out here in the country ... '

The wind changed yet again, carrying the criminals' voices right away, so that no more scraps of their conversation drifted up to George. But she did not need to hear any more: she was frozen with shock. She had heard the important part of their plans, even if she hadn't heard the actual name of the lady whose jewels Karl and Lenny intended to steal. She forced herself to go on keeping quite still a little longer.

At last, the two men down on the beach rose to leave. Craning her neck, George saw them pushing their boat back into the water.

The wind turned again, at just the right moment.

'Now, row straight for the shore,' ordered the thick-set man.

'Right, Mr Karl,' said the redhead.

'Aha,' thought George, 'so the thin one with red hair is Lenny, and the other man, who seems to be the leader of the gang, is Karl!'

She tried desperately hard to get a look at Lenny's face, but twilight was already falling, and all she could see was a pale blur.

The boat was rowed away. George waited until it was quite a long way off before she dared stretch her stiff arms and legs.

'If Julian, Dick and Anne don't find me they'll give up the hunt and start shouting my name,' she said to herself. 'That means the men will hear them and realise the island isn't deserted after all. They may even turn back to make quite sure no one overheard them talking – and if they catch me it won't be much fun!'

A shudder ran through her. Well, the sooner she came out of her hiding place the better, then!

Chapter Three

WHO IS THE GANG'S VICTIM?

George hauled herself out of the hollowed-out ledge and started the difficult climb upwards, clinging on as hard as she could. If she put one foot wrong she would fall right out into space. It was better not to think about that! At last George reached the top of the cliff, her heart beating fast. Phew! She was safe!

Without even stopping to get her breath back, she began running along the path. She was in a hurry to find her cousins.

All of a sudden, coming round a bush, she collided with Julian, who was busy searching every inch of the ground in that part of the island.

'George!' he cried. 'There you are – at last! Wherever were you hiding? Dick and Anne are searching the other side of the island for you, but I had a feeling that this was the right place to look.'

'Oh, Julian, just wait till you hear what's happened!'

Even in the twilight, Julian could see that his cousin looked pale and shaken.

'What's the matter? You look quite ill!'

'No, I'm all right, but I've had a terrible shock. You won't be surprised when I tell you what happened! There *is* something the matter, all right! I'm on the track of one of those mysteries that are always coming our way – so let's go and find the others, and I'll explain it to all of you.'

George and Julian went round the castle, and were soon back on the other side of it. When Dick and Anne saw them they exclaimed in surprise.

'Hullo, there's George!' cried Dick. 'Well done, Julian! Where did you find her?'

'We were just beginning to get worried,' added Anne.

'Julian wouldn't have found me if I hadn't wanted him to,' explained George, out of breath, throwing herself down on the grass. 'In fact I'd already come out of my hiding place when he met me. If I'd stayed there, none of you would ever have found me at all!'

'That's what *you* think!' replied Dick. 'If you were so sure of yourself, why didn't you stay put?'

George scowled. It was easy to tease her – she would always rise to the bait.

'I tell you, you'd never have found my hiding

place, and if I say so you can believe me! You know I never tell lies!'

Seeing that a quarrel threatened, Anne interrupted quickly. She smiled at her cousin and said soothingly. 'Of course we believe you, George, but do hurry up and tell us why you came out of your hiding place in the end!'

George relaxed at once. Certain that she would create a great sensation, she said, in a dramatic voice, 'I've uncovered a plot!'

Her cousins stared at her with open mouths.

'A plot?' repeated Julian. 'What do you mean?'

'I mean, I overheard two members of a gang of criminals discussing a burglary they were planning to commit. Of course it's our duty to stop them – just let me get Timmy untied, and then I'll tell you all about it!'

Timmy's nose had already told him George was back, and he was tugging at his lead and barking. George untied him and patted his head. The dog was so pleased to see her that he almost knocked her down.

'Take it easy, Timmy, take it easy!' she cried, laughing.

Dick and Julian rejoined their cousin, carrying some dry wood. With Anne's help, they piled it up on the paving stones.

'It gets chilly here in the evenings, even in summer,' said Julian. 'We'll light a big camp fire, and George can tell us her story before supper.'

Julian lit the fire, and soon cheerful flames were blazing away in the big courtyard of Kirrin Castle.

'Right, we're listening, George, old girl!' Dick told his cousin, settling down comfortably.

'Yes, do please tell us about it, George!' begged Anne.

'If this is as serious as you think,' added Julian, 'tell us exactly what happened, and mind you don't miss out the slightest detail.'

Sitting cross-legged, with one arm round Timmy's neck, George began her story.

Her cousins were careful not to interrupt. When, at last, she had finished, Julian exclaimed, 'What luck the jewel thieves didn't discover you! As it is, they don't know anything about us, and they must be thinking they can go ahead with their plans quite safely. Well, it's perfectly obvious what *we* ought to do: we must make sure those plans fail!'

'We must tell the police at once!' cried Anne. 'There isn't a moment to lose!'

George shook her head. 'Don't be so silly, Anne! All I know about the thieves is their first names – I don't know where they come from, or even who it is they're planning to rob. It wouldn't be any use going to the police when we have so little evidence. They'd only laugh at us.'

'Then we must at least tell Uncle Quentin. He'll make sure the right people know what's going on!'

'Oh no, Anne, no! Can you see me bothering Father with my story, when he's always so wrapped up in his work? He'd tell me I was being over-imaginative, and he might even punish me for making up stories! You know how strict he is!'

Julian got up and looked at his watch.

'George, you must be quite faint with hunger after all this excitement! I vote we have supper now, and after that we'll hold a council of war. We'll look at the problem from every possible angle, and then decide what to do about it.'

Julian's proposal was passed unanimously, and as soon as they had finished their supper, the Five went back to discussing their plan of action.

'Right!' said Julian. 'Now, what exactly do we know? Two men called Karl and Lenny are planning to attack an unknown woman on July 30th, with the help of a third member of the gang called Dave. Is that right, George?'

'Absolutely right. And it's something to do with a jewel theft, and the victim lives on her own in a manor house. At least, I'm almost sure they said "the lady of the manor", though the wind was blowing rather hard just then.'

'That's something that should help us,' Dick put in. 'I suppose we *are* all agreed that we want to solve this mystery on our own?'

'You bet we are!' replied the other three, in chorus.

The Five stayed up quite late that night. First,

the children and Tim went down to the little beach where the men had landed. They used their pocket torches to search around and see if any clues had been left behind. They did not find anything, but George made her dog sniff around, to get used to the smell of Lenny and Karl, and she let him know that they were bad men and she didn't like them. Once he got the idea, Timmy started barking frantically, with his nose to the ground.

'He understands! Now he'll pick their scent up again if he meets them!' George assured the others.

Then the children went back to their camp fire to decide how to start their investigations.

'First of all,' said Julian, 'we must identify this mysterious "lady of the manor". What manor could it be? It's up to us to find out!'

'There are so many manor houses round here!' sighed Anne. 'One in almost every village – and most of them are simply known as "The Manor"!'

'Yes, and sometimes the "manor" isn't much more than a largish farmhouse,' added Dick. 'That's not going to make our job any easier!'

Julian made himself sound optimistic.

'Well, at least we can leave ordinary small or medium-sized houses and seaside cottages out of it,' he said. 'That's something.'

'So what we have to find,' George went on, 'is a woman who lives on her own in a large house called a manor. And then we must discover whether she has a treasure in the place – a family heirloom.'

'After that,' Anne added, 'we must find out if her heirloom is made of emeralds.'

'And finally,' said Dick, 'once we're sure we know who Karl and Lenny's victim is, we must go and see her and put her on her guard – and then it'll be up to her to inform the police.'

'So then all the police will have to do is set a trap for the thieves and catch them red-handed,' Julian finished.

George was chewing a blade of grass. 'I wonder,' she sighed, 'who the third man is? The one called Dave. He's another unknown factor in this mystery. And I wonder just how he's going to be "in a position" to help Karl and Lenny on July 30th? Oh well – let's go to sleep now! Perhaps we shall see things more clearly in the morning!'

Chapter Four

THE SEARCH BEGINS

The sun was already high in the sky when the Five woke up next day.

The children took turns to go and wash their faces in the stream which flowed from the island's little spring. Then they devoured their breakfast hungrily.

'Got any ideas, George?' asked Dick, with his mouth full.

'For starting our investigations, you mean? You bet I have! I suggest we set to work straight away, and begin by dividing up the coast into sections. Then we pinpoint the loneliest parts, because we're going to find the "manor" we're looking for in some sort of isolated place. We shall have our work cut out for us!'

Julian, the oldest and most sensible of the cousins, thought that George's idea was a very good one. And he agreed that they ought to start work as soon as possible.

'There's no time to be lost,' he explained. 'We only have a couple of weeks to make our inquiries – remember, the date the jewel thieves have fixed for their robbery is July 30th!'

After they had cleared away their breakfast things the Five set off in good spirits, going down the little path leading to the sheltered cove where George kept her rowing boat moored.

'It's a good thing the two men landed on the other side of the island,' she said. 'Otherwise they'd have known it *wasn't* uninhabited just at the moment!'

The children jumped into the boat and rowed towards the mainland. Once they had reached the beach near Kirrin Cottage, they left the boat there and got their bicycles out.

Before they set off, George unfolded a map of the countryside.

'Look,' she said. 'We're here, and there's the coastline, with Kirrin village and all its houses and holiday cottages. It's no use at all looking there! Farther south there's a whole string of little seaside resorts. The only deserted part of the coast anywhere round there is the stretch of moorland they call the Wild Heath. We'd better see if there's an isolated house anywhere there!'

Dick bent over the map.

'The northern part of the coast looks more

hopeful,' he said. 'There don't seem to be very many clusters of houses up there.'

'You're right,' said Julian, tracing the line of the shore with his finger. 'It doesn't look as if there are many towns or villages up the coast until you get to Lighthouse Point, which is some way away from here. Those deserted parts would be just the place to commit a crime!'

Anne shivered. 'Yes,' she said. 'I can see that a woman living alone there would be exactly the kind of victim Karl and Lenny would choose!'

'Well, we mustn't lose any time!' said George firmly, folding up her map again. 'Where shall we begin?'

'We might as well look at the Wild Heath first,' suggested Julian. 'And on our way back we can drop in at Kirrin village for some fresh eggs.'

So the Five set off without any more delay. The children pedalled briskly along the road, and Timmy, who loved a bit of exercise, bounded along beside George. Sometimes he would dart off to left or right of the road, to give himself a longer run – and he frightened quite a few chickens, and sent panic-stricken rabbits scuttling off!

The little party cycled straight through Kirrin village. It was market day, and the old high street looked very pretty in the golden morning sunlight, with its picturesque stalls. The butcher who sometimes provided nice big bones for Timmy looked out and waved.

It was not long before the children reached the Wild Heath – a great, deserted stretch of moorland. It looked very gloomy. Anne glanced timidly round.

'Brr . . . I don't like it here!'

'And we're seeing the Heath in broad daylight, too!' said Dick. 'It must be positively sinister at night! I'm sure there can't be anyone living here!'

'Oh, but there is!' said George. 'I should have remembered earlier. If I didn't, it's because Fitzwilliam Manor is almost forgotten by the local people. No one ever talks about it.'

'Fitzwilliam Manor? You did say "manor?"' cried Dick.

'Yes, and the owner's a woman, too!' George went on. 'But she's a kind of a hermit, poor thing, and not at all rich. I don't think our jewel thieves can possibly be after her.'

'Never mind,' said Julian. 'We must have a closer look at this manor – where is it?'

'Over there. Look!'

A large, dark, square house stood on a rise in the desolate moorland, not far from the children.

'In the old days,' George explained, 'Fitzwilliam Manor stood in the middle of a village. But people all gradually moved away because there wasn't any work for the men to do, and all the houses and cottages crumbled away, except for the big manor house. I don't know any more about it, except that there's an old lady living

A large, dark, square house stood on a rise in the desolate moorland.

Alf was busy repainting his boat.

there now. I'm not sure if she lives on her own or not – all I know is that she's very poor. I can't imagine her owning any jewels!'

'Well, we must go over the Wild Heath with a fine tooth comb!' said Julian. 'Let's see if there are any other lonely houses around.'

But the Five searched the moorland in vain. They did not find any more buildings, apart from the manor house.

'Let's go back to Kirrin,' said George. 'We'll try to find out more from Alf the fisher-boy. He's very friendly, and he'll help us if he can.'

The children set off back to Kirrin, cycling fast. First they stopped among the colourful fruit and vegetable stalls in the village high street to buy some eggs. Then they made for the quay in Kirrin Bay. They found Alf quite easily. He was busy repainting his boat, whistling as he worked.

He grinned when he saw the children. He knew them all well. 'And how have all of you been since last summer?' he asked.

After talking to him about nothing in particular for a few minutes, Julian cleverly brought up the subject of the 'lady of the manor', and asked some searching questions.

'Interested in Mrs Fitzwilliam, are you?' exclaimed Alf. 'Poor old lady – there's nothing much to tell you about *her*. She's lost everything – her husband, her children and her fortune – and she lives in that old house of hers like a hermit. We hardly ever see her in the village. She only comes to do a little shopping now and then. How she manages to live I don't know! She usually comes in on the bus in the morning, and wanders round the village as if she were a ghost. We all feel sorry for her, but she's as unfriendly as her own moorland, and she won't talk to anyone.'

'Well,' muttered George under her breath, '*that*'s going to be a lot of help when we try to get in touch with her, I must say!'

The children said goodbye to Alf, and went back to Kirrin Cottage. Aunt Fanny and Uncle Quentin gave them a good lunch, and then, early in the afternoon, the little party set off again, going north this time.

'We'll never be able to search the whole area we want to cover in a single day,' Julian told the others. 'We must work our way through it methodically! The main thing is to keep our eyes wide open – and not be too impatient.'

North of Kirrin, the country looked very different from the coast south of the village. It was less forbidding and rocky once you got inland, but still it did not attract many visitors, because the steep cliffs and all the rocks offshore made it an uninviting place for boats or bathing. So there were fewer houses along this part of the coast too.

After they had gone nearly a mile, the Five divided into two groups. Julian and Anne made up one group, and Dick, George and Timmy the other. But they searched the area they were covering in vain. All they found were some small farmhouses, with whole families living in them, and a few fishermen's huts, which didn't interest them.

They met again at the end of the afternoon with nothing to report, feeling rather tired. George said she thought they had spent enough time on their inquiries for one day, and it was time to go back to the island. They spent the rest of the day enjoying themselves, bathing and playing games.

'Tomorrow,' Julian told the others before they went to bed, 'we'll go on exploring the countryside and see if we can find the house we want.'

Chapter Five

FITZWILLIAM MANOR

So, early in the morning the children set off due north. They bicycled through the part of the country they had explored the day before, and once again they divided into two teams to carry on with their investigations. This time the Five were luckier. When they met again about mid-day, at the spot where they had arranged to have their picnic lunch, they were all in a triumphant mood.

With her usual enthusiasm, George was the first to cry, 'Victory! Dick and I may have discovered who Karl and Lenny's mysterious victim is!'

'Victory for us too!' cried Julian, in the same tone. 'Anne and I have heard of another woman living alone, and she could easily be the one we're after!'

Both teams gave details of their discoveries.

George and Dick had seen a large, grand-looking house through some trees.

'I asked questions about it of some of the local people passing by,' Dick explained, 'and apparently a lady called Mrs Grant lives in the house all on her own. It's called Manners House – and when she heard that, George agreed with me that Karl and Lenny might have been talking about "Manners House" and not a "manor house" when she overheard them.'

'Yes,' agreed George. 'The wind had changed just at that moment, and I could only hear scraps of what they were saying.'

'Anyway,' Dick went on, 'this Mrs Grant seems to be very rich, so it's quite likely she owns some valuable jewels.'

Now it was Julian's turn.

'What we discovered wasn't exactly a manor,' he said, 'but it's called Manor Farm. It looks like a fine, prosperous place, and the farmhouse is a big one. I was lucky enough to meet the postman, and I asked him some questions. He didn't mind telling me what I wanted to know. The place belongs to a woman farmer called Mrs Langley. She's very efficient, but something of an eccentric, and she employs farm workers who don't live on the farm itself – they come to work there in the morning and go home in the evening. So she could easily be our "lady of the manor" – the one the jewel thieves are planning to rob.'

George frowned thoughtfully.

'That makes three possible "victims" already,' she sighed. 'And we're only just beginning our inquiries! It looks as if this could be rather complicated!'

The Five sat on the grass to eat the picnic they had sensibly thought of bringing with them, and then they went on with searching the countryside, going farther north all the time.

It took them three more days to explore the whole district. By then the children had worked their way right up the coast to Lighthouse Point. But, oddly enough, they found no more lonely houses which might have been the isolated 'manor'. There were just those three they had discovered on the second day of their investigations.

That evening, sitting around their camp fire on Kirrin Island, they took stock of the situation.

'I was afraid we'd be looking for a needle in a haystack,' said George, 'but I'm rather more hopeful now. We've ended up by finding that there are only three women who are likely to be burgled by Karl and his accomplices. That's Mrs Fitzwilliam of Fitzwilliam Manor, Mrs Grant at Manners House, and Mrs Langley of Manor Farm.'

'Yes, that's right,' Anne agreed. 'So now we must find out which one of them owns the jewels, and then warn her of the danger, and that will be that!'

'I think we can leave Mrs Fitzwilliam out of it,

don't you?' said Dick. 'She seems to be as poor as a church mouse.'

'Hold on!' Julian told him. 'You know, we can't be quite sure how well off she is! Some rich people pretend they're poor, so as to put off burglars and people who want to sponge on them.'

'Right!' said George. 'The best way to find out, as soon as possible, if we can cross Mrs Fitzwilliam off our list is to go and see her first!'

And so next day the four children and Timmy set off 'on the trail', as Dick put it, yet again.

They made for Fitzwilliam Manor on the Wild Heath, hoping to talk to the 'lady of the manor'. As they were passing through Kirrin Anne suddenly saw some lovely flowers for sale outside the gate of one of the cottages.

'Oh, do let's stop for a minute!' she begged the others. 'I want to buy some of those roses for Aunt Fanny. Your mother is so kind to us all, George! We can leave the bunch of flowers at Kirrin Cottage for her on our way back to the island.'

And she ran towards the tempting bunches of flowers, while the others waited for her. But suddenly a frail, timid-looking old lady stopped just in front of Anne. She was frightened by the roar of a motorbike coming straight towards her. Anne could guess that the poor old woman did not know whether to step forward or back, so she quickly pulled her back on to the pavement, just as the rider of the motorbike was about to run her down in the middle of the road. Trembling all over, the old lady stammered out a shy, 'Oh, *thank* you!' and then she disappeared among the crowd.

Anne bought the flowers, and then hurried to rejoin her cousin and her brothers. The four of them all mounted their bicycles again and pedalled away fast, with Timmy running alongside. They were cycling along the deserted road when a large bus swept past them, raising a cloud of dust.

'I hate those great big buses!' said George. 'They even frighten the cows!'

Julian laughed. 'But they come in very useful for people who don't have cars or bicycles!' he said. 'Come on, cheer up! We're nearly there.'

Quarter of an hour later, the children got off their bicycles outside Fitzwilliam Manor. George marched boldly up to the enormous doorway of the house, and pulled the rusty chain which hung down within her reach.

The sound of a bell ringing sent echoes all through the house.

'Oh dear, there's nobody in,' sighed Anne, after they had waited in silence for a while.

But as if to contradict her, a little spyhole opened in the big door, and a woman's voice, quavering with old age, asked, 'What do you want?'

Julian stepped forward.

'We'd like to see Mrs Fitzwilliam,' he said politely, 'on very important business!'

'I never see anyone,' said the voice.

'Oh, please, Mrs Fitzwilliam!' cried George impatiently. 'It's only for your own good!'

'Go away! I don't know you!'

And the spyhole closed again. The children looked at each other, taken aback.

'Well, *I* don't know!' muttered Dick. 'That's what comes of trying to help people!'

The sound of the spyhole being opened again interrupted him.

'That little girl – yes, the one over there – why, I do believe I recognise her!' said the voice. 'Fancy that! Come over here, my child – yes, it really *is* you! You helped me down in the village just now. Oh, dear me! I was so upset that I hardly even thanked you properly! Come in! Come in, children, do!'

She had changed her tune so suddenly that the children were still rooted to the ground! But immediately the door was opened wide, and there stood Mrs Fitzwilliam. Sure enough, she was the same fragile little old lady that Anne had helped not long before. And but for Anne's kind act, the timid 'lady of the manor' would never have agreed to let strangers into her house – she was so used to keeping herself to herself.

The Five found themselves in the big sitting room of Fitzwilliam Manor. It was a gloomy room,

46

though it still showed traces of past glories.

George, who had been telling her story, was just coming to the end of it. Mrs Fitzwilliam did not for a moment doubt anything Uncle Quentin's daughter might say. George's father was well known in these parts as a famous scientist.

'Yes – oh, dear me, I might have known it! Oh, yes, I do have a treasure! A real family heirloom!' Mrs Fitzwilliam admitted, to the surprise of the children. 'And you say burglars are planning to steal it? Oh, how dreadfully rash I've been to keep it in the place! It isn't safe under my roof – I know that now!'

'Please don't worry, Mrs Fitzwilliam,' said Julian, feeling sorry for her. 'They aren't planning their burglary until the end of the month, so you'll have plenty of time to warn the police.'

'Yes – oh, yes, you're quite right. Really, sometimes I don't know if I'm on my head or my heels! I'm on my own too much, you see, with only my memories for company. But I'll take your advice, my dears. And now, would you like to see my treasure?'

The children were delighted to have discovered the jewel thieves' victim so soon, and they were touched to think that Mrs Fitzwilliam trusted them enough to tell them about her family heirloom, and even show it to them. They were happy to follow her, and Anne, who loved pretty things, was delighted to think she was going to see the fabulous emeralds.

Mrs Fitzwilliam guided the Five through a great many rooms, and down corridors which seemed to be endless, until at last they reached a room with bare walls and no furniture in it. The children looked at each other in surprise. There was no sign of any treasure here!

The lady of the manor saw the expression on their faces, and smiled.

'I can guess why you're so surprised,' she said. 'But you see, I couldn't leave my treasure out in a place where anyone can see it! Now, watch this!'

She pressed a tiny flower bud which stood out from the carving on the mantelpiece. The mantelpiece itself swung round, revealing the door of a little secret room.

'Come in, my dears, and admire my treasure!'

The children followed her in, after George had instructed Timmy to 'stay'. The old lady had lit an oil lamp, and now she proudly held it up to show them a full-length portrait of a victorious knight in armour.

'That is my ancestor!' Mrs Fitzwilliam told them. 'Sir Eustace Fitzwilliam of Fitzwilliam! My most precious treasure! That painting is beyond all price.'

At first, the Five could not believe their eyes. But then they realised what had happened. George had told her story of the criminals in such

'That is my ancestor!' Mrs. Fitzwilliam told them.

a hurry that she had only mentioned a 'treasure' and a 'family heirloom', forgetting to say that they were after some jewels, and in fact they had mentioned emeralds. That was why Mrs Fitzwilliam had misunderstood!

Dick bit his lip hard, so as not to burst out laughing. Anne looked at the knight in armour, in silence. George was scarlet with embarrassment. Julian realised it was up to him to put things straight. So he explained to Mrs Fitzwilliam that no one was trying to steal her ancestor's portrait, and the criminals were after a jewel case containing some precious stones.

Mrs Fitzwilliam seemed to be relieved. She said she was very pleased to have met the children, and after they had collected Timmy she showed them their way back to the gate, asking them to come and see her again some time.

The Five found themselves on the Wild Heath again – and no farther on with their investigations than before. They got on their bicycles and started off down the road.

'Well,' said Dick, 'that was a real waste of time, if you like!'

'Not entirely,' said Julian. 'It does at least mean that we can cross Mrs Fitzwilliam off our list of possible victims!'

Chapter Six

MANNERS HOUSE

The children decided to carry on with their investigations that afternoon, and went to see Mrs
Grant at Manners House. When they had reached
the big house, which had a gate with upright bars
like the railings in the wall round its grounds, they
got off their bicycles and rang the bell beside the
gate. The front door of the house opened almost
at once, and a tall, athletic-looking woman
appeared at the top of the steps. She walked
slowly towards the children.

'What do you want?' she asked, in a rather unfriendly voice.

'Good afternoon,' said Julian politely. 'Can we
see Mrs Grant?'

'I am Mrs Grant.'

'We wanted to talk to you – about something
important. May we come in?'

Mrs Grant frowned. She looked suspicious.

'I do not usually open my gate to complete strangers, even if they're only children,' she said ungraciously.

Julian quickly introduced himself and the other children by name. 'And you're quite right to be careful, Mrs Grant!' he added, smiling. 'I mean, you live alone, and so –'

'How do you know I live alone?' snapped Mrs Grant, interrupting him.

'We found out that you did,' Dick explained.

'I don't like the sound of that at all, young man! You go "finding out" things about me, you know that I live alone – and you expect me to let all four of you in? Not to mention that dog. It looks savage to me!'

'Timmy's as gentle as a lamb!' George said, bristling. 'And he's ready to defend you too, if you'd like him to!'

'Or to go for my throat if you say the word!'

'How can you say a thing like that?' cried Anne, choking with anger. 'You've got quite the wrong idea – we've come to warn you about a gang of thieves, and – '

But Mrs Grant would not let her go on.

'And how do I know you're not part of a gang of thieves yourselves?' she replied. 'Although I think it's more likely you're trying to play some sort of practical joke on me, and not a very good one. Go away, children!'

Julian protested.

'Honestly, Mrs Grant, we aren't thieves or practical jokers either – just the opposite! If you don't want to let us in, well, never mind – we'll stand out here and tell you about it. But do *please* listen to us!'

'I don't have any time to waste, you young scamps, so kindly get out of here!'

The children tried to make Mrs Grant see reason, but she wouldn't change her mind. It was their own time they were wasting!

'If you don't go away this minute,' Mrs Grant warned them, 'I shall set a dog on you, and he's twice the size of yours. My nephew has come to visit me today, and he's brought his dog Sultan with him!'

At that moment, a young man wearing a polo-neck sweater appeared at the top of the steps.

'What's going on, Aunt Laura?' he asked. He was holding back an enormous Alsatian by its collar.

'Oh, nothing much,' Mrs Grant told him. 'Just some impertinent children trying to get into my house. I have an idea they may be spying out the lie of the land for a real gang of thieves!'

The Five – including Timmy! – let out such an indignant howl of protest that the Alsatian barked back at them. 'Woof!'

Timmy was quick to reply. 'Woof! Woof!'

The Alsatian and his master came down the steps to join Mrs Grant.

'Open the gate just a little way,' the young man suggested to his aunt. 'Let Sultan show these kids his teeth, and he'll soon make them run for it, just like rabbits.'

Mrs Grant hesitated. 'Do you really think so, Mark?'

But Mark had already opened the barred gate himself. Obviously, he had not expected Sultan to be so excited by the sight of strangers that the dog would break away from him. With a sudden tug, the enormous Alsatian freed himself, and made for the nearest of the 'intruders'. It was George!

But Timmy was not going to let him reach his target – he made for the other animal, and there was a fierce and terrifying dog-fight! The animals were both growling, and the children were screaming. The two grown-ups tried to drag Sultan back inside the gateway.

George was the only person who was not frightened.

'Go on, Tim! Just you show that great big brute!'

At last, Mark managed to grab the Alsatian by the collar. George flung her arms round her gallant defender's neck and kissed him on the nose.

'Now do you understand?' shouted Mrs Grant. 'Go away at once, or you'll be sorry!'

Without stopping to argue any more, Julian signalled to the others to follow him. When the children and Timmy (who was feeling quite pleased with himself!) were some way from the big house again, they sat down by a large rock to discuss the situation. George had looked carefully at Timmy to make sure he wasn't hurt, and her mind was set at rest. He moved so nimbly that the other dog's attempts to bite him had failed.

Dick was blazing with anger.

'Honestly, that Mrs Grant is as stubborn as a donkey!' he cried. 'And talk about being suspicious! To think we only went there to help her!'

'Well, since we didn't get a chance to talk to her properly,' said Julian, in a serious voice, 'the best thing we can do is write to her and warn her about the danger threatening her.'

'No, let's just leave her to stew in her own juice!' said Dick, still boiling over with indignation at the way they had been treated. 'Who cares if she does get burgled? It'll teach her a lesson!'

Anne, who always liked to be on good terms with people, agreed with Julian, and said she thought they ought to write to Mrs Grant. But George did not agree. She had an idea of her own.

'We must carry on with our investigation, and make sure we do it thoroughly,' she said. 'If we wrote her a letter she might not reply, and then we shouldn't know what to think. So that wouldn't get us anywhere! No, come what may, we must get in touch with Mrs Grant herself and talk to her!'

And George, fearless as ever, told her cousins her plan.

'I'll see to it!' she declared. 'Judging by what Mrs Grant herself told us, her nephew and his dog are only there on a visit. They'll have gone again this evening, so then I'll go back and ring the bell by the barred gate, and I'll talk to Mrs Grant myself.'

Julian objected strongly.

'You're crazy!' he said. 'She won't even listen to you!'

'We'll see about that. Anyway, I can always try!' George was determined.

'It's a mad idea, George! I shan't let you. I'm the eldest. Aunt Fanny entrusted you to me, and it's up to me to make sure you're safe. Suppose you go back there and Sultan hasn't left after all? No, I forbid you to do any such thing, George!'

'Oh, all right, all right! Don't get so worked up! We'll just write her a letter, then, as you suggested.'

Once they had made up their minds to write to Mrs Grant, the children left Anne's flowers for Aunt Fanny at Kirrin Cottage and went back to Kirrin Island again. They felt very hungry after the day's adventure. Anne cooked a large meal of sausages and tomatoes over the fire, and all the children ate it eagerly. Timmy was hungry too and wolfed down the big bowl of dog food which George prepared for him. They were very tired, but tomorrow they must go and see Mrs Langley at Manor Farm.

Chapter Seven

A NIGHT-TIME ADVENTURE

Lying in the tent she shared with Anne, George waited for her cousin to fall asleep. The boys were asleep already, in their own tent. Without making a sound, George slipped out of the canvas tent, and Timmy came up to her, quivering all over with delight.

'Ssh!' she told him in a whisper. 'Whatever you do, don't bark! Come on! We're off on an expedition, just the two of us!'

The dog followed her in silence. Side by side, in the bright moonlight, the two friends went down the path leading to the cove where the boat was waiting in the dark. George jumped into it.

It had seemed as if she were giving in and agreeing to do as Julian said, but really she was only pretending. George had made up her mind to try talking to Mrs Grant again. 'Come on, then, Timmy, off we go!'

Side by side, in the bright moonlight, the two friends went down the path leading to the cove.

Poor George had fallen into a trap set for burglars!

The dog was already on board the boat. George took the oars and rowed smoothly to the shore of the mainland. The sea was calm and there was a warm breeze. Timmy seemed to be enjoying his outing.

George pulled her boat up on to the beach near Kirrin Cottage, fetched her bicycle, and set off along the road northwards, pushing the pedals down as hard as she could. Timmy trotted along beside her, pleased to be going on this unexpected adventure with her. They heard the church clock strike eleven in Kirrin village. Its sound was carried to them by the wind.

'Good!' thought George. 'Mark is sure to have gone home by this time. But Mrs Grant may not be in bed yet, and with luck perhaps she'll agree to let me in, if she sees I'm on my own. As for you, Timmy, you must stay out of sight.'

Once outside the barred gate of Manners House, George jumped off her bicycle and told Timmy to lie down behind a bush.

'You stay there till I come back!' she said. 'Good dog, Timmy!'

Then George went up to the gate. She could not see any lights on inside the house. She rang the bell, but she could not hear any sound. She thought that Mrs Grant had probably disconnected it, so as not to be disturbed in the night. Feeling very annoyed, George wondered what to do next. She wasn't going to have come all this way just for nothing! Suddenly she had an idea.

'Why don't I climb the gate? Then I can go right up to the house and bang on the door. I shall make so much noise that I can't possibly be accused of trying to slink into the place secretly for some underhand reason!'

No sooner said than done! After making sure that the gate really was closed and locked, George started to climb it. Nimble as a cat, she reached the top and then slid down on the other side. And then disaster struck!

She had hardly reached the ground when she tripped over a wire running through the grass. The wire must have been connected to an alarm bell, because next moment a loud ringing sound was heard inside the house! Poor George had fallen into a trap set for burglars!

She quickly jumped up, rather dazed, muttering under her breath about her bad luck. But she had hardly gone another step before the door of the house was opened, and bright light flooded the garden. Mrs Grant appeared at the top of the steps! She was wearing pyjamas and a dressing gown, and her threatening attitude was not very reassuring. She was holding a stout stick with a metal tip.

'Who's that?' she called brusquely.

Hobbling slightly, George came forward.

'It's only me, Mrs Grant – one of the children who visited you this afternoon,' she explained calmly. 'I just *had* to see you, whatever happened. And since your bell wasn't working – '

'Stop making excuses!' snapped the owner of Manners House. 'I knew you children were up to no good, all along!'

'Truly, you've made a mistake!' George told her desperately. 'I'm only here for your own sake! Listen, my father is Mr Kirrin, the well-known scientist, and – '

'And how am I to know you're really his daughter? Would he go letting you wander around alone at night, without anyone to keep an eye on you?'

'I can explain everything,' George began. 'Please believe me! All this is just a dreadful misunderstanding. If only you'd agreed to listen to us earlier – '

'I'm not feeling any more like listening to you now!'

And with these words, Mrs Grant came up to George, seized her arm and shook her roughly, taking no notice of her protests.

'Come along, girl! You might as well admit that you came here to scout around the place! You must belong to some criminal gang, and you were hoping to tell them the lie of the land here. But as you can see, I'm not so easily taken in! The house and garden are full of burglar alarms. You were out of luck!'

'You've got the wrong idea, honestly you have!'

cried George, beginning to feel really scared now. 'My cousins and I only came here to put you on your guard. There *is* a gang of criminals, and they're planning to steal your treasure!'

'Treasure? What sort of story are you making up now? Good gracious, you'd say anything at all just to make me let you go, wouldn't you?'

'No, I wouldn't!' replied George, indignantly. 'I never tell lies!'

'Except to me! Just why should I believe you? The facts speak for themselves. You've broken into private property by night, in secret. That's against the law! Tomorrow morning I shall call the police and they'll come up here to fetch you. Until then I'm going to shut you up somewhere. A night spent cooling off, and thinking of what you've done, will be very good for you!'

It was no good for George to go on protesting that she was innocent. Mrs Grant just wouldn't listen to her.

Holding the little girl's arm in an iron grip, the owner of Manners House dragged her to the garage.

'I'd lock you in the cellar,' said Mrs Grant, 'but you might kick up a row and stop me sleeping. Out here, you can scream and shout to your heart's content, and I shan't hear a thing. And even if I did –'

This time George's fear gave way to anger.

'You can't do this!' she cried furiously. 'I

haven't done you any harm!'

'Only because I didn't give you a chance! Go on, get in there! And it's no use trying to soften me up!'

'Some day you'll be sorry you misjudged me like this!' shouted George. 'But it may be too late then!'

Quite beside herself, George struggled frantically to escape from her enemy's grasp. But Mrs Grant was a strong, athletic woman, and the girl could not take her by surprise. She kept holding her victim in the same steely grip, and despite George's resistance, she was pushed into the garage beside the house. Mrs Grant locked the garage door.

'And tomorrow the police will deal with you!' she said.

George heard her walking away, and bit her lip ruefully.

'I'm in a nice mess now!' she muttered. However, she was not going to admit she was beaten yet. She looked carefully all round her prison. It was no use. Apart from a tiny air inlet for ventilation, there was no way out of the garage except through the door. George was a prisoner!

But while George was helpless in the garage, looking in vain for some way of escape, what do you think her dog was doing?

Timmy was a highly intelligent dog. He adored George, and instinctively understood her. If she was feeling sad, he would try to cheer her up. If she was in a happy mood, he would gambol around, sharing her pleasure. And in the same way, he could guess when she was in danger. As well as being devoted to George, he was very fond of Julian, Dick and Anne. Timmy's job was to protect George and her cousins, and he did it very conscientiously, and very bravely too if necessary.

In the normal way Timmy was an obedient dog, who did everything his young mistress told him to, so when George had said he was to stay behind the bush and wait for her, he understood exactly what she meant.

Ears pricked, he followed the little girl's movements as she climbed the barred gateway of Manners House. Then he heard the noise of her fall, and the sound of the alarm bell, followed by Mrs Grant's loud, angry voice. All this had worried him badly. And when George shouted her protests of innocence he could tell, from the tone of her voice, that she was in trouble.

Now Timmy's instinct told him to disobey orders for once and leap to his little mistress's aid.

But it was no good trying to jump over the gateway. The barred gate was much too tall!

It looked as if he could not possibly get in.

Without wasting time barking, which would have been pointless, Timmy tried to squeeze through the iron bars of the gate, but he was too big. He took a run and tried to jump the gate!

Still no use! Every time, he fell back before he could even reach the top of the gate. Maddened, he watched Mrs Grant drag George off to the garage, and then he started to growl softly with helpless rage and desperation.

No one heard him. He tried jumping yet again, but it was hopeless. After locking George up, Mrs Grant went back into the house. Realising that his little mistress was a prisoner, Timmy uttered two or three short, sharp barks. 'Woof! Woof! Woof!'

George heard him. Her heart thudded with hope.

'Tim!' she shouted as loud as she could. 'Is that you, Tim? Help, Timmy! Help!'

Poor George knew very well that dear old Timmy could not set her free. All the same, just knowing he was there and could hear her voice gave her a little courage.

'Whatever happens, I must get out of here!' she told herself. 'I shall look pretty silly if Mrs Grant hands me over to the police tomorrow morning – what a fuss there will be! I can just imagine Father flying into a rage. And how he'll scold us for wanting to make our inquiries all by ourselves! What's more, the story is sure to leak out somehow, and then the thieves will be warned, so they'll probably decide to give up the idea of this burglary and go and commit another crime somewhere else, and we shall never be able to catch them!'

Meanwhile, Timmy had realised it was no use at all for him to try getting past that barred gate. His doggy mind suggested a very simple line of reasoning to him.

'George is a prisoner,' he told himself, 'and I can't get her out, so I must go and warn the others!'

And with one last glance at the garage where George was shut up, Timmy immediately turned round and ran off as fast as he could go.

Chapter Eight

TIMMY TO THE RESCUE!

Timmy ran on for a long time at a steady pace, without ever straying from the route he was taking, until he reached the beach near Kirrin Cottage. Then he stopped for a moment. What should he do now? George's parents were there in the house, very close. He was sure they would hear him if he barked loud enough.

But Timmy had a vague feeling that that would not be the best thing to do. Waking Julian, Dick and Anne was a better idea!

To do that, however, he would have to get back to the island. Good old Timmy did not hesitate for a moment! The sea between the shore of the mainland and Kirrin Island stretched out ahead of him in the moonlight. He jumped into the water. Struggling against the current, he swam bravely on, spurred on by the thought of George in trouble.

When he finally set foot – or rather paw! – on

the sandy beach of the little cove below the castle, he hardly even stopped to shake himself. He climbed the steep path and dashed into the boys' tent, barking like mad.

'Woof! Woof! Woof! Woof!'

Julian and Dick woke with a start.

Sitting up in bed, Dick opened his eyes very wide.

'Timmy! Whatever is the matter? Have you gone off your head? Why are you barking like that?'

Julian, who was more clear-headed, realised at once that something was wrong.

'The girls must have had some kind of accident!' he cried. 'Otherwise George would never let her dog bark like that!'

The two boys jumped up and ran out of their tent. The girls' tent was perfectly quiet. There was nothing moving inside.

'George! Anne!' called Julian, going up to it. 'Is everything all right?'

Timmy rushed into the girls' tent, barking as hard as he could. The boys heard Anne's sleepy voice.

'Oh, George, do stop Tim barking like that!'

Dick shrugged his shoulders and caught Timmy by the collar.

'Shut up, will you?' he told the dog sternly. 'What's the idea, waking people up in the middle of the night? Hi, George – can't you make this

mongrel of yours keep quiet?'

But it was Anne, not George, who suddenly emerged from the tent. The little girl seemed to be terribly worried.

'Oh, Julian – Dick! George has disappeared! I thought she was sound asleep beside me, but I've just seen that there's no one there. Oh dear! Why is Timmy barking like that? I'm frightened! Something awful must have happened to George. I can feel it! I'm sure of it!'

'Don't be so silly!' replied Dick roughly. 'George must have gone for a walk, and Timmy's seizing his chance to fool about!'

Julian did not agree.

'Don't be so silly yourself!' he told his brother. 'If George had gone for a walk she'd have taken Timmy with her.'

'That's right!' Anne backed him up. 'George and Timmy are inseparable. Oh, Julian, I'm so frightened! Where can she have gone?'

'Let's search the whole island,' suggested Dick. 'We'll soon find her.'

They started by calling George's name, but Timmy was impatient. He did not want them to lose any time. Tugging at Julian's pyjama jacket and leaping about in front of him, he rushed to the path leading down to the cove. Julian, Dick and Anne followed him, feeling very worried.

As soon as the children saw that the rowing boat was not there, they realised that George had left Kirrin Island. But why hadn't she taken Timmy with her?

It was only then that Dick noticed that the dog was all wet.

'Timmy *did* go with her!' he cried. 'But he swam back to the island!'

The children looked at each other in alarm. They guessed that some disaster must have happened on the mainland, and brave Timmy had crossed back to the island to raise the alarm. Quickly, Julian came to a decision.

'I can guess what's happened!' he said. 'George must have wanted to try talking to Mrs Grant again after all – and more than likely she got into trouble. We must go and help her as fast as we can.'

'Yes – but how?' asked Dick, completely at a loss, while Anne burst into tears. 'We haven't got a boat now, so that means we're stuck here on the island!'

'Don't talk such nonsense, Dick!' said Julian impatiently. 'I can do just what Timmy did for George! I'll swim ashore. Then I'll come back for you with the boat, Dick, and we'll bicycle to Manners House.'

'I want to come with you too!' said Anne, her voice tearful but still firm. 'I'm sure I can be of some use, and so can Timmy!'

'Woof!' Timmy agreed.

'Perhaps we'd better not leave you on your own,' said Julian.

'You will be careful, Julian, won't you?' Anne begged him.

'Yes, of course. Now, while I'm gone, you two get dressed, and have my clothes ready for me – and don't forget to bring our torches!'

Timmy was wagging his tail now. He watched with interest as Julian waded into the cold water and struck out for the mainland. The intelligent dog realised that he was going to help George.

Julian found that the sea was not as icy as he had feared. Swimming with a powerful crawl, he made for the shore, his mind full of his cousin. Ought he to tell Uncle Quentin and Aunt Fanny or not?

'Not straight away,' he said to himself. 'Uncle Quentin is so strict! Perhaps we may never have to tell him about it at all.'

He came to shore on the beach near Kirrin Cottage, feeling glad of the bright moonlight, which meant he could see the boat pulled up on the beach only a couple of paces away. As he had expected, George's bicycle was missing from the hut.

Julian pushed the boat out, jumped into it and started rowing towards the island.

A little later, the rowing boat was making for the mainland again, with Julian, Dick, Anne and Timmy on board. The dog's nose was pointing forward. He seemed to be impatient to reach land.

Once they were on shore, Julian, Dick and Anne got straight on their bicycles and rode off towards

Manners House. Timmy ran silently along beside them. Good old Tim did not feel at all tired. Anne had rubbed him down with a towel, so he was not cold either.

'We must be going the right way!' Julian soon decided. 'See how fast Timmy is running! All we have to do is let him guide us.'

The little party pedalled hard until they reached Manners House, where they dismounted. Timothy had already run up to the barred gate. He was looking in the direction of the garage, and he let out a short bark. 'Woof!'

A muffled voice replied to him. 'Timmy! Good dog, Timmy!'

Dick sighed with relief, and then shouted back. 'George! George, it's us! Where are you?'

'Here, in the garage! Quick, let me out!'

Julian interrupted.

'If we go on shouting like this, we shall be sure to wake Mrs Grant – unless she's awake already!' Then, quite loud, he said, 'Shut up, George!'

The children listened hard for a moment in the silence that fell around them.

Inside her prison, George remembered hopefully what Mrs Grant had told her. 'You can shout to your heart's content, and I shan't hear a thing.' Perhaps the owner of Manners House was a little hard of hearing, or else she slept with her windows shut!

Clustering outside the barred gate, Julian, Dick,

Anne and Timmy were still listening. But nothing seemed to be moving inside the house. Julian heaved a sigh of relief.

'Right. Everything's all clear! But stop being such donkeys, and let's work in silence. We've got to get George out of there!'

'That's what I say, too,' Dick agreed. 'But how?'

'Let's think.'

'It strikes me,' said Anne, 'that the first thing to do is climb this gate. Come to think of it, that's what George may have done herself.'

'If so,' remarked Julian, 'it didn't do her much good – as we can see!'

'There may be an electric fence, or a burglar alarm, or a man-trap of some sort,' suggested Dick.

'This gateway isn't electrified, and if George had been hurt by a man-trap she wouldn't be able to shout so loud,' said Julian. 'But your idea of a burglar alarm sounds quite likely to me, Dick, so let's be very careful. I'll climb the gate first, and take care to drop on the gravel path and not on to the grass. On the pathway you can at least see what you're treading on!'

Thanks to this precaution, Julian climbed the barred gate successfully. Once safe on the other side, he told Dick to join him. 'You stay outside with Timmy, Anne,' he said. 'Then, if we get taken prisoner too, you can go back to Kirrin Cottage for help.'

Anne did not feel very assured as she watched

her brothers going along the path which led to the garage, on the other side of the gate.

When they reached the small building the boys scratched at the door. 'George, it's us – Dick and Julian! Is this door the only way out?'

'Yes,' replied George. 'There's no other opening at all that's big enough, and the door's locked. I've found some tools in the boot of Mrs Grant's car, but I can't manage to force the lock.'

'Blow!' said Dick. 'Any ideas, Julian?'

Julian thought for a moment, and then looked up.

'The garage has a tiled roof,' he said. 'If I can just manage to get some of the tiles off, George can get out that way.'

'Brilliant idea!' exclaimed Dick, under his breath.

Julian put his mouth close to the door.

'George – climb up on the car and give the tiles just above your head a gentle tap. We're going to get you out through the roof!'

'I see!' said George, quickly grasping his plan.

Then Julian asked his brother to give him a leg up to the garage roof. The tiles were large, flat, and easy to remove. Julian did not have much difficulty in taking several of them off the roof, placing them beside him as he went along. Soon he could see his cousin's face raised to his in the moonlight.

'Hullo, old girl! Well, you certainly got yourself into a fix! But for Timmy, who swam across to the island and came to wake us, you might have stayed here till you died of old age!'

'Good old Timmy!' George grinned. 'And good old all of you, too!' she added, smiling. She was deeply touched.

Julian lay flat on the roof and helped his cousin to scramble up beside him. 'Now, give me a hand putting these tiles back!' he said.

George burst out laughing. 'I can just imagine Mrs Grant's face when she finds the bird has flown!' she said. 'She'll see that the door's still locked, so she'll never be able to make out how I got away!'

A couple of minutes later, Julian and George rejoined Dick. Anne was waiting impatiently on the other side of the gate. When the two boys and George had climbed it, Timmy hurled himself at his mistress and flung her to the ground in his joy at seeing her again. George hugged him hard.

'Tim, darling old Tim! You saved my life! And so did the rest of you! Thank you – oh, thank you!' As usual, she was exaggerating a little, but her cousins didn't mind.

'We'd better get out of here fast!' Julian advised, when Anne had hugged George in her turn. 'You can tell us all about it as we cycle home, George!'

George and her cousins mounted their bicycles, and left Manners House as fast as they could.

Back on the island, the children held a council before getting some well-earned rest. Each of them had a different explanation for Mrs Grant's attitude, but they were too tired to be able to think clearly, so at last they decided to put off the rest of the discussion until next day.

Chapter Nine

MANOR FARM

Next morning, in broad daylight and with a good breakfast inside them, the children found them. they could see the situation more clearly than the night before.

They had woken up rather late, but after sleeping off last night's adventure they felt fighting fit again.

'So now,' said Julian, 'let's try and make sense out of it all! You know, George, it was a great mistake to go breaking into Mrs Grant's place like that. It wasn't in the least necessary, especially since we'd decided to write to her. On the other hand, your misadventure does mean that we were indirectly able to get the information we needed!'

'What do you mean?' asked Anne, in surprise.

'Well, didn't we want to know if Mrs Grant was the owner of the treasure Karl and Co. are planning to steal?'

'Yes, of course!'

'Now we know! Because George did manage to talk to Mrs Grant, and though it wasn't the friendliest of conversations, it throws some light on things for us. Mrs Grant can't own the emeralds! If she did, she wouldn't have been so surprised and angry when George mentioned her "treasure". She certainly seemed to think that George was making up the whole story!'

'You're right,' cried Dick. 'So now we needn't go back to Manners House any more. Mrs Grant isn't the woman the thieves are planning to rob!'

Julian noticed that George had not said anything. She seemed to be deep in thought, sitting on a rock with one arm round Timmy's neck.

'Hi, George!' said Julian, laughing. 'Come back down to earth and join us, won't you? You haven't listened to a word of what we've been saying!'

'Yes, I have,' replied George. 'I heard it all. Only – I'm not quite sure that I agree with you.'

'Why not?' asked Dick, looking very surprised.

'I don't think Mrs Grant's reactions prove for certain that she doesn't own the emeralds.'

'But if she did,' Anne objected, 'she'd have believed your story, and she'd have been alarmed. Surely she'd have thanked us for warning her of the burglary the criminals are planning?'

'Unless,' objected George, 'she really *did* take us for young members of their gang, who'd been given the job of getting information out of her!

That could be why she didn't seem to know any-thing about the treasure – just pretence, to dis-courage thieves from trying to rob her. It would have been the best way to lead us astray!'

The four children argued for a little longer, without coming to any definite conclusion. Julian wound up the meeting by saying, '*I* think the best way is to go on trying to cross names off our list. We had three possible victims, and we've already crossed Mrs Fitzwilliam's name out. If you like, we'll put a question mark against Mrs Grant. Now let's go and visit Mrs Langley, and after that, we'll see!'

'Right!' cried George, jumping up. 'I'm all in favour of immediate action! Let's start off for Manor Farm!'

The children realised that it was a very tricky business, investigating this particular mystery. George had only seen two of the three criminals, and they knew almost nothing about them. They had not set eyes on any emeralds, themselves, and they still did not know who the victim of the robbery was to be!

'If only people would be a little bit helpful,' said Anne, bicycling along the road to Manor Farm with the others, 'things would be so much easier!'

But the children seemed fated to find that the people they wanted to help weren't at all willing to talk to them. In fact, Mrs Fitzwilliam had been suspicious, and Mrs Grant had been hostile, but it turned out to be absolutely impossible to speak to Mrs Langley at all!

When the children entered the farmyard of Manor Farm, a girl coming out of the dairy told them that 'the missus' never saw any visitors – Mrs Langley was a businesswoman first and foremost! She told her farm workers what jobs to do, as well as running the business of selling her farm produce herself.

'Just now she's getting ready to go off in the van delivering eggs and poultry. If you want to see her, you'll have to phone and make an appointment, if she's willing to give you one – and that's not very likely!' added the girl, laughing. 'She devotes all her time to her business, you see.'

At that moment the engine of a Land-Rover was started up in the yard. There was a woman at the wheel.

'There she goes,' the girl told them.

'Hi! Mrs Langley!' shouted Julian, waving his arms. 'Wait a moment, please!'

The Land-Rover slowed down, and the woman at the wheel turned her thin face to look at the boy.

'What do you want?' she asked in a forbidding tone.

'We want to talk to you, Mrs Langley,' said Julian. 'It's important!'

'On business?'

'No – no, it's something personal.'

'I haven't got time.'

And that was all she said. Before the children had recovered from their surprise, Mrs Langley had stepped on the accelerator and disappeared in a cloud of dust.

'Well!' gasped Anne in amazement. 'You couldn't say *she* was very friendly!'

'I told you so,' said the young dairymaid. 'Well, it's time I was getting back to work.'

She was just turning away when another farm worker appeared. He was a man with a pleasant, round, smiling face.

'Did you want to see the missus, then?' he asked kindly.

'Yes, we did!' replied George, annoyed by the way Mrs Langley had spoken to them. 'We had something very urgent to tell her – in her own interests, too!'

The man began to laugh.

'Something in her own interests, eh? She should've listened! There ain't no one keener on her own interests than what she is! The missus is fair rolling in money, but she's a bit of a miser, you know. Hereabouts, they do say she has no end of money in the bank, and a treasure down in her cellar too! She thinks as how no one knows about that treasure, but there ain't a living soul as hasn't heard of it!'

Pricking up their ears, the children tried to find out exactly what Mrs Langley's 'treasure' was supposed to be. But the farm worker couldn't tell them any more. He was sure that 'the missus' *did* have a treasure, but what sort of treasure it was nobody knew!

When the Five got back to Kirrin Island, about mid-day, they held a big council of war, sitting looking out at the sparkling sea.

'I really do think we're on the right track now,' said Julian. 'The "lady of the manor" who owns the emeralds, and who is to be the jewel thieves' victim, certainly isn't Mrs Fitzwilliam. And there's not much chance that she's Mrs Grant. It's far more likely that they're planning to burgle Mrs Langley at Manor Farm.'

'Yes, that's true,' George agreed. 'But the trouble is, we can't be *sure* it's safe to cross Mrs Grant off our list. So we still have two possible "victims". And since neither of them is willing to talk to us, and we don't know absolutely for certain which of them is in danger, we can't get the police to step in yet!'

'That's right,' agreed Dick, gloomily. 'If we tipped the police off ourselves we'd just look silly! You've got to admit this is a bit much! Trying to help someone who's doing all she possibly can to *stop* you helping her!'

'Yes,' sighed Anne. 'People can be very unco – unco –'

'Operative!' Dick finished for her.

'Meanwhile,' said George, summing it all up,

'we'll have to solve this case by ourselves! We must keep watch on Manners House as well as Manor Farm. It looks as if the near future isn't going to be very restful!'

Sure enough, over the next few days the Five had a great deal to do. The job of watching the two houses was a tiresome one, and since they weren't quite certain who the intended 'victim' was, they felt that they were not really getting anywhere. Of course, they had no more news of the thieves themselves. The Five spent most of their time divided into two teams, watching the surroundings of Manners House and Manor Farm, in the hope of picking up some kind of clue.

They did make another attempt to visit Mrs Langley and explain what it was all about, but that was no good. She flatly refused to see them!

And then, just when they were beginning to get tired of the whole business, things began to happen!

Chapter Ten

ON THE THIEVES' TRAIL

'Well, I suppose it's a good thing we have the rowing boat and our bicycles to get us about the place!' said Dick at breakfast one morning.

'And a good thing Timmy's paws don't wear out!' muttered George gloomily.

'And a good thing we're on holiday,' said Julian, 'with plenty of free time!'

'I'm starting to think that all this about jewel thieves and precious stones is just a bad dream!' sighed Anne.

The children were fed up. Time was passing, and there were not many days left before 'Operation Emeralds'! The Five still had no idea who the mysterious Dave was. Of course, they could not keep watch on Mrs Grant's house and Mrs Langley's farm both day and night, so they were afraid of missing a chance of coming upon Karl or Lenny prowling around the future scene of the crime. That would at least have told the children where it was – and what's more, then they could have tracked the criminals down to the gang's headquarters!

That morning Anne realised that they were running short of provisions on the island. They were right out of cocoa and butter, and they had hardly any sugar or biscuits left!

'And we need potatoes, matches, eggs and a couple of lettuces,' Anne told the others. 'Oh yes, and some sardines too!'

'Quite a shopping list,' remarked Julian.

'Let's go and stock up in Kirrin,' suggested Dick.

George pushed her boat out into the water, and the Five got on board, with their shopping baskets. Over at Kirrin Cottage, the children fetched their bicycles and then set off along the road, with Timmy as escort.

They knew they could get some provisions from Aunt Fanny, but there were some things which they needed to get from the shops. Julian and Dick went into the general store. Anne bought some freshly-baked bread from the baker's shop before she went into the greengrocer's. George, of course, went into the butcher's shop, which also sold eggs, because she knew that the butcher would find a large juicy bone for Timmy. It was as she came out to join the others who'd already finished their shopping that she was jostled by a man who did not even stop to say he was sorry. She turned round angrily to point out what he had just done, but then she suddenly stopped dead. The man was thin, and red-haired, and his figure reminded her of a man she had seen before, or rather had glimpsed briefly – Lenny, Karl's accomplice!

She swallowed the angry remark she had been going to make. Luckily the red-haired man was taking no notice of her!

George went up to her cousins.

'See that red-headed man over there?' she asked them. 'I wouldn't swear to it, but I do believe that's Lenny – one of the criminals!'

Julian, Dick and Anne jumped. George was obviously in a state of great excitement, and they could tell she wasn't joking.

'Gosh!' exclaimed Julian. 'George, if you're right we mustn't lose sight of him. He's the clue we weren't even hoping to find any more – something to put us on a really useful trail!'

'Yes!' agreed Dick enthusiastically. 'Let's follow him! He may well lead us to Karl.'

'Always supposing he really *is* Lenny!' George reminded them.

'Even if he doesn't lead us to Karl, at least we might find out where he lives himself,' said Anne.

'Unless he has a car here,' sighed Dick. 'I can hardly see us travelling hard on the heels of a racing car, on our bicycles!'

'Racing cars haven't got any heels!' said Anne. 'Do try to talk properly, Dick!'

'This is no time for squabbling, you two,' Julian interrupted them. 'We'd do better to keep a close eye on our man.'

The crowd of idlers had gone away again. The red-headed man was walking back towards the baker's shop. It was a warm sunny day, and the baker's wife had put a couple of tables and some chairs outside on the wide pavement so that people could sit down and have something to eat and drink. The man sat down at a table where there was already another customer – a sturdy, thick-set man, with his hair cut very short.

'It's him! It's Karl!' whispered George in triumph. 'So I was right!' she went on. 'There are our two thieves, both together. Our luck has changed at last!'

'So long as we don't let it get away from us,' Julian corrected her. 'Or rather, so long as we don't let those two rascals get away from us!'

'But how do we shadow them without letting them see us?' asked Anne.

'For a start,' said George, in a low voice, 'I'd just love to hear what they're saying now – and come to think of it, that's easy! We only have to sit down next to them. They don't know us at all, and I don't suppose they'll suspect children our age of anything.'

So saying, she followed Lenny, along with

Timmy, without waiting to hear what the others thought. Her cousins followed her. They sat down at the empty table right beside the one where Karl and Lenny were sitting.

Just as George had expected, the two men took no notice whatever of their young neighbours.

They were in deep conversation, talking in low voices. What they were saying would have sounded harmless enough to anyone who wasn't in the know, but the children *were* in the know! And they didn't miss a word.

'So Dave arrives tomorrow, Lenny? Are you sure?'

'Yes, Mr Karl. He'll be starting his job straight away – rather earlier than we expected.'

'In that case, maybe we could put the date forward?'

'No, Mr Karl, better not. The 30th is the best date, as we all agreed before. We've already fixed all the arrangements for our getaway, and –'

'Not so loud, Lenny! I'm not deaf.'

'No, Mr Karl. I was saying that . . .'

The red-haired man's voice died away to an inaudible murmur. The four children glanced at each other. They were full of curiosity about Dave, wondering exactly what his job was.

Obviously they dared not exchange comments out loud, so they had the idea of writing them down on scraps of paper which they passed round to each other. Anyone watching would have

thought they were simply playing some kind of pencil and paper game.

'Dave may be a gardener Mrs Grant's just engaged,' suggested Dick.

'No,' Julian scribbled back, 'I think he's more likely to be a new man coming to work at Manor Farm.'

'How can we find out?' wrote Anne.

'We mustn't lose sight of these two for a moment!' replied George, in a very firm pencil scrawl.

They had reached this point when Karl and Lenny rose from their table. Julian and the others, who had been sensible enough to pay for their Coca-Cola in advance, copied them. They left their own table very inconspicuously.

'The man-hunting season is now open!' muttered Dick in fierce, mock-dramatic tones.

'Shut up, idiot,' replied his brother. 'The most delicate part of the whole operation is just beginning!'

As for Timmy, for the last moment or so he had been showing, in his own way, that he recognised Karl and Lenny too! George had made sure that he got to know the scent of the criminals after they left Kirrin Island, and had told him they were bad men. So now, coat bristling slightly, nose pointed forward, Timmy was only waiting for a signal from his mistress to leap at them! But instead George held him back and made him keep quiet.

93

'Later, Tim. Quiet, now! Don't attract their attention!'

Timmy was rather surprised, but all the same, he obeyed. If it had been left to him, he would happily have gone for the men's throats. His instinct told him they were up to no good.

Pretending to be innocent passers-by out for a walk, the Five set off to follow Karl and his accomplice. They were careful to keep a close watch on the two men and they never lost sight of their prey. As for the two thieves, they were obviously in no hurry.

They walked along the main street with the children and Timmy still shadowing them. But then, much to the annoyance of their pursuers, they shook hands and said goodbye. Karl entered a tobacconist's shop, while Lenny went on his way.

Julian came to a quick decision.

'Anne and I will follow the red-headed man,' he told them. 'The rest of you keep an eye on Karl. We'll meet at the boat as soon as possible. Those who get there first wait for the others.'

'Right,' said George. 'See you soon.'

Julian and Anne went off after Lenny. George and Dick, left behind along with Timmy, pretended to be admiring the lighters on display in the tobacconist's shop window.

Lenny was walking fast. Julian was tall for his age, and had long legs, but he still found it difficult to keep up with him. Anne, walking beside him, had to break into a trot now and then to keep up at all. She was beginning to get breathless. Julian was worried. His sister couldn't keep this pace up for very long. What was more, with Anne half running like that, they were bound to attract the attention of their prey some time!

However, Julian went on walking, frowning hard and pretending to be in a great hurry himself, just in case Lenny turned round. But Lenny did not look back once. All the evidence seemed to show that he hadn't got the faintest idea he was being followed.

Julian and Anne, still in pursuit of him, left the village. Anne, who was out of breath, whispered to her brother, 'Do you think this is going on much longer? Where is that man going to lead us?'

Julian was wondering the same thing. If Lenny set off along a deserted country road, it would be impossible for his pursuers to go on following him without being noticed.

Suddenly Lenny stopped. They saw a big motorbike leaning up against a tree. Lenny went up to it, took off the padlock, and mounted the bike. Julian made a face. This was what he had been most afraid of, and now it had happened! The criminal had motor transport!

'We can't follow him now!' sighed Julian. He stopped, and thrust Anne into the cover of a hedge.

'All we can do is take down the number of his motorbike.'

*   *   *

Meanwhile Dick, with his nose pressed to the window of the tobacconist's shop, was trying to get a sight of Karl inside it.

'Don't be such an idiot!' growled George. 'He'll notice you! Just wait till he comes out again!'

They did not have long to wait. The stocky man soon appeared in the shop doorway. He was busy filling an evil-smelling pipe, and he did not even see the children. Timmy growled quietly.

'Ssh!' George whispered. 'Not a sound, old boy!'

Karl walked up the main road again at a leisurely pace. George and Dick had no difficulty in following him. All they had to do was keep strolling along and chatting to each other, looking as if they were taking an interest in the shop windows from time to time.

All of a sudden Karl disappeared through the doorway of an old barn which George knew had recently been converted into flats. She quickened her pace.

'Just suppose he lives here!' she murmured. 'Hurry, Dick – take a look at those cards with people's names on them!'

The children quickly found what they were looking for. A small piece of cardboard in one of the little metal frames said, 'Karl Braun, Flat 3b'.

'Well, whether that's his real name or a false one, at least we know he's living here!' cried George triumphantly. 'Quick, let's go and tell the others about it, Dick!'

The Five arrived at the boat almost at the same time. Julian and Anne confessed that they had to give up following their man, and then congratulated George and Dick on trailing Karl so successfully.

'This means,' said Julian, summing it up, 'that now we shall always know where to find one of our suspects. However, we haven't got any evidence against him yet, so it's going to be some time before we can really start crowing!'

Chapter Eleven

DAVE TURNS UP AT LAST

'Today is July 28th!' said Dick out loud, on the morning of that date. 'And we're still not much farther on than we were at the very beginning! The day after tomorrow, Karl and Lenny will go into action, and we still don't know who their victim is going to be. What *can* we do?'

'The simplest thing,' George decided, 'would be to follow Karl, and start shouting for help as soon as he and his accomplices start breaking into Manor Farm or Manners House, whichever it is!'

'It's risky,' said Julian.

'I – I think I'll be rather frightened,' confessed Anne.

'Coward!' Dick told her.

'Don't let's quarrel!' George begged them. 'The trouble is that Karl, who seems to be the leader of the gang, may easily have decided not to take part in the actual burglary himself.'

99

'That would be just our luck!' sighed Dick. 'Then we'd have spent all our time watching him for nothing!'

'Obviously, it would be best if we could have found out who Dave is first,' said George. 'Because apparently the gang can't go into action without him. Well, we still have two days' breathing space. Some helpful new clue may turn up yet!'

George was speaking more truly than she knew. She had been given a whole pile of letters by her father, to be taken to Kirrin to the post, and she was just coming out of the post office when a telegraph boy stopped her.

''Scuse me,' he asked her politely, 'but I'm new in these parts – I've only been here a few days. I've got two telegrams to deliver, and I can't find out where the addresses are. I shall get into hot water if I bring the telegrams back undelivered!'

George smiled. She rather liked the look of the boy.

'Well, I live here,' she said, 'so I'm sure I can help you. What are the addresses?'

The boy read them out loud. 'Marmaduke Chamberlain-Smith, Paterson Place, and John Davidson, Honeysuckle Cottage,' he said.

George knew the people who were to receive the telegrams slightly, and she told the boy where they lived. He thanked her, and added, with a laugh, 'Marmaduke Chamberlain-Smith! Fancy having to get your tongue round that every time you told someone your name! John Davidson doesn't sound so odd to me – but maybe that's because my own name is Dave! Well, I'd better be on my way!'

He mounted his bicycle and rode off, whistling, leaving George standing on the pavement as if turned to stone.

'That boy's name is Dave,' murmured George to her dog. 'Did you hear that, Tim? And he himself said he'd only been working in Kirrin for a few days! He must be the gang's mysterious accomplice!'

That very evening, as night fell, the Five took stock of the situation after a long discussion.

'Putting all the pieces of the jigsaw together,' said Julian, 'I think we can see what the thieves are going to do. They'll get Dave to deliver a telegram to their victim – one which will make her leave her house. Then, while she's safely out of the way, they'll break into the place and steal the emeralds. It's as simple as that!'

'Then all we have to do now is shadow Dave the whole time,' suggested Dick. 'In the end we're bound to find out where he's delivering that telegram!'

But though they spent the next day in a state of feverish activity, the children got no positive results. It was all very well for them to take turns trailing Dave about the place – they did keep watch on him the whole time, as Dick had suggested, but nothing came of it.

Dave had only a few telegrams to deliver, and none of them were to women living alone. They were all addressed to families visiting Kirrin for their summer holidays, and staying in the holiday cottages in the village. He never went near either Manners House or Manor Farm – and they were both in the Kirrin postal district.

'This is hopeless!' said Anne that evening when the Five met again, after the post office had closed. 'It looks as if nothing is going to happen at all!'

'Which would be nice and reassuring,' muttered George, 'if only we weren't certain that something *is* going to happen!'

July 30th saw the Five preparing for action at their camp on Kirrin Island.

'It's today or never!' announced Dick, washing in the island's little stream, with much splashing of cold water.

'I just hope,' said Julian, drying himself energetically, 'that we'll be able to step in at the right moment this evening. What a pity we still know so little about what exactly is going to take place!'

When Kirrin Post Office opened up that morning, the Five had been waiting outside for some time. They did not want to run the risk of losing sight of Dave. They knew that they must follow all his movements even more closely than before, now that the day itself had come.

At this time of the year the village was busy with

summer visitors so the Five shadowing Dave were able to move about among the crowds without being noticed. Dave rode round on his bicycle, and it was quite easy for them to follow him.

That morning Dick was the first to shadow the telegraph boy when he started work. The others waited outside the baker's shop, where they had home-made lemonade and lovely fresh scones, with lots of butter and passed the time by playing a card game.

'Nothing to report!' Dick told them, when he got back. 'Dave delivered a telegram to Mrs. Jones's boarding house, and another one to a fisherman's family down at the harbour, and that was all!'

George jumped up from her chair.

'My turn to follow him now,' she said. 'See you soon!'

But Dave did not come out of the post office again straight away, and when he did emerge, it was only to deliver a single telegram right in the middle of Kirrin village.

The rest of the morning passed uneventfully, and so did the afternoon. Dave never once even looked like setting off on the road northwards, and he still never went anywhere near either Manners House or Manor Farm. The Five were at their wits' end.

'We must have made a mistake, that's all,' sighed Julian, after the post office had closed for the day. 'Dave has nothing to do with the criminals after all. It's another Dave who's their accomplice, one we don't know about. We've wasted precious time following that telegraph boy – and now it's too late to do anything about it!'

'I'm not so sure we did make a mistake,' said George firmly. 'Look here – we're not giving up now! We don't want to have to think we spoilt our hols by spending our time shadowing people and watching houses all for nothing! And something tells me that luck is coming our way at last!'

'Well, it'll have to hurry up about it, old girl!' grunted Dick. He was in a bad temper. 'Meanwhile, we'd better get on Karl's trail straight away. He's the only possible clue we have left to lead us to the scene!'

But unfortunately Karl did not seem to be at home – Dick was actually bold enough to ring his doorbell to make sure.

'There's no more time to lose!' cried Julian. 'We must snatch a quick bite to eat, and then go and keep watch on Manor Farm and Manners House. It's the last chance we still have of stepping in to save the day!'

Yet again, the Five found themselves bicycling northwards. Once they were near the two lonely houses, they divided up into two teams once more. Julian and Anne went to take up their position near Manor Farm, while George and Dick set off for Manners House.

Chapter Twelve

TROUBLE AT MANOR FARM

For the first time since the start of the adventure, the children felt that their hearts were not really in it. They had been wrong to suspect Dave the telegraph boy – suppose they were wrong to watch Mrs Grant's house and Mrs Langley's farm too?

Even if something did happen at one of those houses, how were they going to prevent the thieves getting away with their loot, now that they were divided up like this? Two children against three men – the odds were not too good!

'Oh dear!' thought George. 'If only the "victims" had been less suspicious and more understanding!'

As for Julian, his thoughts were gloomy ones as he crouched behind a bush near Manor Farm, while twilight fell round him. The boy felt responsible for the younger children. He was beginning to blame himself, and to feel sorry he had not insisted on George's telling her father what was going on.

'But Uncle Quentin is always so wrapped up in his scientific calculations – I dare say he wouldn't even have heard me!' he told himself, to salve his conscience. 'He's always telling George she's imagining things. Anyway, it's too late to do anything about *that* now.'

Beside him, Anne changed her position, and a twig cracked under her feet.

'Don't make any noise, Anne,' said her brother. 'You'll give us away.'

'Who to, I wonder?' sighed Anne, shivering slightly. 'There isn't anyone about.' That was quite true. It was pitch dark now. Mrs Langley's farm workers had gone home, and the whole place seemed to be asleep.

Julian and Anne waited in the shadows. They both felt depressed. They were waiting, yes – but what for? And would the thieves really be coming to burgle Manor Farm? They felt weighed down by uncertainty and a vague feeling of helplessness. Though they were usually such energetic, enthusiastic children, they were feeling thoroughly downcast as they kicked their heels in the dark. They weren't even frightened.

Julian was surprised by his own lack of excitement, and as for Anne, she was amazed at her own calmness.

'What a nuisance!' she whispered suddenly.

'We can hardly see a thing now. I think we're too far from the farmhouse to be able to keep watch properly. Suppose we went a bit closer?'

'It isn't very wise,' said Julian, surprised by his sister's unusual daring himself. 'Still, we can try!'

Julian and Anne had posted themselves by the ditch facing the gateway of Manor Farm. They were well hidden there, but it was true that they could not see very much through the thick bushes which gave them cover.

'The best thing would be to get inside the farmyard itself,' Julian decided. 'I can see a big farm cart beside the hen-houses. Now, if we got underneath it –'

Anne had some misgivings, but as she was the one who had suggested moving closer, she dared not object.

'All right. I'll follow you.'

Without a sound, Julian began to creep forward in the dark. Crouching low, he crossed the road, with Anne close behind him.

The gateway of Manor Farm was closed, and in theory the stout fence all round the buildings should have kept anyone from getting into the farmyard.

However, after prowling around the outside of the fence to see what it looked like, Julian and Anne found a place where part of it was torn away. It was quite easy to get in through this gap.

Soon, the brother and sister were inside the

farmyard. Everything was silent round about.

'There's the cart!' whispered Julian. 'Now to get underneath it!'

'We shall get dreadfully dirty,' murmured Anne, who was very neat and tidy. 'Why don't we hide behind those huts instead?'

'You idiot! Those are the hen-houses. If by a stroke of bad luck you –'

But it was too late! Anne was already running incautiously towards what she had called the 'huts'. Her foot bumped into some invisible obstacle. She tripped and fell forward, flinging out her hands to save herself – right against a hen-house door! Immediately a rooster, woken up with a start, uttered a loud 'Cock-a-doodle-do!'

His crowing was followed by a tremendous uproar. The hens, roused as well, started fluttering about like mad. They cackled and squawked and flapped their wings – the noise would have woken the dead!

'Oh, gosh!' exclaimed Julian, in alarm. 'That was all we needed! Mrs Langley will be down on us like a ton of bricks now. Let's get out of here as fast as we can! Honestly, how clumsy can you be, Anne? Bother those stupid birds! If only that wretched rooster would stop stirring them all up!'

Panic-stricken at the sound of the hubbub she had started, Anne clung to her brother's arm as he hurried her towards the gap in the fence.

But the children had no time to get away – a

bright light was already shining on them, while two men, who looked very threatening, were running towards them.

'You young varmints! Got you now!'

'Thought no one had noticed you prowling round the farm, did you?'

The men had grabbed Julian and Anne and were shaking them roughly. They were both talking, taking turns, without even giving their prisoners a chance to explain.

'Got in through the gap in the fence, eh? As if Mrs Langley was the sort to let people break into her property! She was the one who spotted you first and told us to make that gap!'

'Her idea was to make things easier for you and then catch you red-handed!'

'In the act – or rather, in the hen-house! I suppose you were after her poultry!'

'Certainly not!' Julian finally managed to protest, indignantly. 'We're not thieves!'

'And what would you call people who get into other folks' poultry yards by night to wring their fowls' necks, then?'

'I'm not a bit interested in these chickens!' cried Julian. 'My sister startled them when she tripped over a stone, that's all.'

'And just what were you doing here in my farm-yard?' asked Mrs Langley's voice suddenly.

She had just emerged from the house and was coming towards them.

'It strikes me you're rather inexperienced burglars!' she said sarcastically. 'When you tried to approach me the other day I smelt a rat immediately. And seeing you ferreting around outside the farm a little later, I knew you were up to no good. So I asked two of my farm workers to keep a watch here for a few nights. I guessed you'd end up by breaking into my property and getting caught!'

Julian's eyes were blazing with rage. To think they had gone to all that trouble to try and protect Mrs Langley in spite of herself, and now *she* was accusing *them* of being thieves!

'You're quite wrong, Mrs Langley!' he cried. 'We're not thieves! We were only here to defend you in case anyone tried to burgle the house – and there *is* a gang of criminals plotting to do exactly that, at least we think it's you they want to burgle! They're going to do it tonight, too. We came the other day to warn you!'

Anne was crying. She could not say a word. She was thinking that this was very like George's misadventure when she was caught by Mrs Grant. And now it was Anne's turn to be in trouble herself! This business of the jewel thieves and the emeralds looked like turning into a disaster!

Making a great effort, she managed to stammer, 'We – we really didn't mean to do anything wrong. I promise you we didn't!'

'I don't believe you,' said Mrs Langley coldly.

'I'm going to telephone the police, and they'll come and question you.'

Julian was in despair. He was not so worried about the police. Once they knew who he was, they could hardly suspect him of wanting to wring Mrs Langley's chickens' necks. But the light flooding the farmyard, and the sound of voices breaking the silence of the night, could only put Karl and his accomplices to flight if they were still anywhere near. He felt sure the criminals would abandon the idea of their burglary, and that would put an end to the Five's hopes of catching them!

So the boy tried to convince Mrs Langley, as fast as he could, of the danger.

'Tell your men to go on keeping watch, and to stay in the shadows and be perfectly quiet!' he told her. 'If it isn't too late, and we haven't already frightened the thieves off, maybe they'll fall into the trap yet! And with so many of us here we shall easily be able to overpower them!'

Mrs Langley laughed in his face.

'What an inventive mind you have, boy!' she said. 'Well, you can tell the police this fairy tale of yours in a moment, and we'll see if *they* feel like believing you.'

And despite the children's protests, she had them brought into the farmhouse, where she phoned the police. At the other end of the line, the police sergeant told her that he and his men would come at once, and would be there in less than quarter of an hour to interrogate the suspects and get the truth out of them.

'Then we'll take the young rascals off your hands, ma'am,' said the sergeant, 'and you'll be able to sleep easy!'

Chapter Thirteen

THE THIEVES ATTACK

Meanwhile, near Manners House, George, Dick and Timmy were waiting motionless in the shadows to see if anything happened.

Dick was not really expecting anyone to come trying to burgle Mrs Grant's house. George, however, was biting her nails impatiently. She felt instinctively that the big moment was coming. Suddenly, Timmy stiffened. George gently pressed his nose to tell him to keep quiet.

'Watch out, Dick!' she said under her breath. 'There's someone coming.'

Sure enough, a shadowy figure appeared on the path – and weren't those two more figures, just disappearing into the bushes beside the path?

'Watch out, Dick!' George repeated.

Dick looked at the figure walking towards them, and was rooted to the spot with amazement. It was none other than Dave, the telegraph boy! So

George had not been wrong after all! Dave really was Karl and Lenny's accomplice! And it really was Mrs Grant's house they were intending to burgle!

George and Dick stood perfectly still in the dark, their hearts beating fast. What was going to happen now?

Dave made for the barred gate – and rang the bell! A light went on above the steps. Mrs Grant appeared at the front door.

'Who's that?' she asked.

'Telegram for you, ma'am. With a receipt for you to sign, please.'

Grumbling under her breath, Mrs Grant came down the steps and walked up to the gateway. She looked suspiciously at Dave. Of course, anyone could have got hold of a telegraph boy's cap and bag. But only a genuine post office employee could deliver a telegram and ask her to sign an official receipt.

Mrs Grant could see the yellow telegram and the receipt slip in the light from her house. They both looked quite genuine, but the light here was not bright enough for her to write her name. And then, she might want to send a reply.

'Just wait a moment, will you, and I'll open the gate,' she said. While she went to fetch the key, Dick and George looked at each other. They realised that Dave's job was not, as they had thought, simply to get Mrs Grant away from her house – he was actually going to make her open the gate for him.

What were the children to do now? Shout a warning to Mrs Grant? But suppose she didn't believe them? And it would mean the thieves would attack them, too, and that would do no one any good! No, it would be better to wait, and look for a good moment to intervene.

Mrs Grant came back, carrying the key, and opened the gate.

Then everything happened so fast that George and Dick were left gasping for breath.

No sooner had the owner of Manners House opened the gate to let Dave in than he threw a blanket over her head. At the same moment, Karl and Lenny emerged from the shadows and attacked the poor woman. In no time, they had tied her up and were dragging her to the house. The children heard Lenny's mocking voice.

'So sorry, lady, but we have to tie you up – I'll bet you weren't expecting anything like this! Now, now, don't be so vicious! Stop kicking my shins! You thought your burglar alarms would protect you, eh? But we know our business all right! And we rather fancied walking straight in at the front gate, without having to go to the bother of breaking into the place!'

'Shut up, Lenny,' interrupted Karl. 'Don't talk so much – give me a hand here instead!'

Dick and George watched the sinister trio disappear into the house with their victim.

George thought quickly.

'Listen, Dick!' she told her cousin. 'There's no time to lose. Get on your bicycle and ride straight to the police station. Then come back with some good strong reinforcements! It's the only way to save Mrs Grant and her emeralds!'

Dick hesitated.

'What are you going to do, though?'

'I'll stay here with Timmy and watch the thieves. If by any chance they leave before you get back with the police – well, I'll try to follow them.'

'That's awfully dangerous.'

'We'll see.'

'They may have some kind of motor transport.'

'I didn't hear the sound of a car engine – oh, for goodness' sake, don't argue, just *go*, and hurry up about it! Cycle as fast as you can! Timmy's here to protect me if necessary.'

Dick no longer hesitated. He mounted his bicycle and rode off as fast as possible.

Once she was alone, George couldn't resist temptation. Instead of staying in the shelter of the trees, she came out of her hiding place and made her way cautiously towards the gate.

Though she listened hard and kept her eyes wide open, she did not see or hear anything. The quiet house might have been asleep again. The thieves had switched off the light over the front steps. It was very dark. George was really worried.

Suppose the three men got away with the emeralds before the police turned up to stop them?

Dick was pedalling along the road like mad. He hated to think of his cousin all alone, so near to those dangerous criminals. George could be so foolhardy! The boy wished he was already on his way back to the big house, along with several policemen.

'I'm sure the police will drive me back there in their car,' he told himself. 'Once I've raised the alarm we'll be at Manners House in no time. The main thing is to get to Kirrin as fast as possible!'

The police station was just outside the village. Dick arrived there drenched with perspiration, breathless but triumphant. He had made the journey in record time! But unfortunately, Fate had played a nasty trick on him. He rang the bell and then hammered on the door of the police station, but no one replied. What could be going on? He was still hammering noisily on the door, hoping someone would hear him and answer it, when a window was opened near by. Dick looked up, and saw a man leaning out of a window in the house next door.

'What do you want, boy?'

'I wanted to see the police sergeant, sir. You'd think there wasn't anyone here!' said Dick, annoyed.

'There isn't, so there's no need to carry on like that any longer. The sergeant and the other men on duty were called out to Manor Farm. It's something urgent. I was chatting to them when Mrs Langley telephoned from the farm – that's how I know.'

'Manor Farm? Mrs Langley?' repeated Dick stupidly. Suddenly he felt very worried. 'But why?'

'Thieves after her chickens, apparently! If you want to find the police, boy, you'll have to cycle to Manor Farm. Well, good luck!'

The window closed again. Dick stayed there for a moment without moving, as if rooted to the spot. His thoughts were whirling round and round.

Luck was certainly not on his side tonight. All the police gone – and called to Manor Farm!

Dick shook himself. Gritting his teeth, he jumped on his bicycle again, and set off the same way he had come. But once he reached the place where the road forked, he turned left to Manor Farm instead of right to Manners House.

Once he was in sight of the farm, Dick saw that all the lights were on in the farmhouse. He thought that Julian and Anne must be kicking their heels somewhere out there in the dark, keeping watch, though there was no point in it. He had no time to look for them now. The most urgent thing was to find the police and raise the alarm.

Dick jumped off his bicycle and dashed inside the farmhouse – its door, which was wide open, seemed to be positively inviting him in. But he

'And who might you be, young man?' the sergeant asked.

They drove off fast towards Manners House, taking the three children with them.

suddenly stopped in alarm at the hall doorway. What a shock he got!

The police were certainly there – but so were Julian and Anne, standing in front of the policemen as if they had been accused of some crime!

'Anne! Julian!' cried Dick, rushing into the room. 'What's going on?'

'We're suspected of trying to steal chickens!' Julian told him, with a wry smile. 'It's ridiculous!'

'Oh, Dick! Do hurry up and tell them who we are!' Anne begged him. She was crying.

The police sergeant turned to Dick, frowning heavily.

'And who might *you* be, young man?' he asked.

It took Dick quite a long time to explain the whole story. For a moment he thought the police were about to arrest him too! But at last the sergeant decided to listen to him, since his account of what was going on agreed with the story his brother and sister had told.

Mrs Langley was listening with interest, too. She thought the boy sounded as if he were telling the truth.

'Please,' Dick begged the policemen, 'please, you've *got* to believe me! Do you think I'd have come here, walking right into the lion's den, if I wasn't speaking the truth? We must hurry back to Manners House. My cousin George Kirrin may already be in danger there, and Mrs Grant certainly is! And you have a wonderful chance of arresting three criminals at once!'

The police did not hesitate a moment longer. They quickly said goodbye to Mrs Langley, and then drove off fast towards Manners House in their car, taking the three children with them.

Chapter Fourteen

THE EMERALDS AT LAST

However, with all these delays a great deal of precious time had been lost.

Seething with impatience as usual, George just hadn't managed to keep still for long. After leaving her hiding place, she had made her way to the gateway of Manners House. She found that the thieves had not bothered to close the gate after them.

Unable to stay quietly in the background any longer, she marched in through the gateway, with Timmy at her heels. Her heart was thumping, but she was not afraid. Her curiosity made her go on!

George stopped a little way from the house itself. She was close enough now to see that some light was shining through a crack in the drawn curtains of one of the ground floor windows.

Timmy stood quite still beside his mistress, all his senses on the alert. George took a deep breath and whispered, 'Come on, Tim! Let's scout around the place!'

She went even closer to the house, and reached the window of the lighted room. Very cautiously, perched on the concrete edging of a flower bed, she managed to get her face up to the bright crack which allowed her to look into the room.

What she saw made her heart beat faster than ever! Karl, Lenny and Dave were all there, standing round a chair, and Mrs Grant was tied to the chair.

The window was not quite shut, and George could hear the owner of Manners House speaking in a firm voice.

'Coward!' she was saying to the jewel thieves. 'That's all you are! Three of you, attacking a defenceless woman!'

'We're not here to discuss that sort of thing,' Karl interrupted. 'Where's the jewel case with those emeralds of yours in it? Come on, out with it!'

'I have no idea what you're talking about,' said Mrs Grant scornfully. 'I order you to untie me and leave this house at once!'

Lenny burst into mocking laughter.

'It's no use trying to bluff, lady!' he said. 'We're very well informed. We know quite well that you have a jewel case here, containing the famous emeralds Queen Victoria gave your ancestor. You see, you can't hide anything from us! So come on out with it – tell us where that jewel case is!'

'Since you're so well informed,' replied Mrs Grant, '*you* should know where it is. Go on, look for it yourselves!'

'Well done!' thought George. 'That woman has guts! Oh, Tim, if only you could see the burglars' faces. They look so funny!'

In the dark, Timmy wagged his tail, ready to leap at the men if George gave him the word.

Inside the room where the drama was being acted out, Karl uttered a growl of rage.

'If you don't tell us where those emeralds are hidden you'll be sorry for it!' he said.

'We know how to make you talk,' added Dave.

'Well, go on and try it!' said Mrs Grant, in a steady voice.

'You may be stubborn, but so are we!' Lenny told her.

'That's enough talking for now,' said Karl. 'We'll search the house – and if we don't find anything, it will be the worse for you.'

George saw the three men leave the room. Inevitably they started by searching their victim's bedroom up on the first floor.

'Now then, Timmy, old boy,' said George, 'this is the moment to act! You stay here. I'm going in.'

Suiting her actions to her words, she climbed in through the window, as quietly as possible. She saw Mrs Grant staring at her, wide-eyed. George put a finger to her lips.

'Ssh!' she said. 'Don't make any noise!'

'Here in this lonely house,' said Mrs Grant, ironically, 'I could howl the place down and no one would hear me. Those criminals know *that*, since they didn't gag me! I suppose you're one of their accomplices. I was quite right to be suspicious of you!'

'Hush, Mrs Grant! Don't talk so loud. No, you're wrong,' George assured her. 'I really was telling you the truth the other day, but you just wouldn't believe me.'

Mrs Grant looked George straight in the eye, and suddenly she realised that the girl really wasn't lying to her. Not so long before, she had treated George as an enemy, while all the time the brave child only meant to help her! Mrs Grant was quick to apologise. 'Yes – yes, I do believe you now,' she whispered. 'But it's too late. Quick, you must go away! Those dreadful men might catch you.'

George smiled. She was not a bit afraid.

'No, I'm staying,' she said. 'That's what I'm here for – to set you free. Don't worry! My cousin Dick has gone for the police, and I hope they won't be long.'

As she spoke, she had taken a penknife out of her jeans pocket. She went over to Mrs Grant to cut the ropes tying her to the chair.

'No,' said Mrs Grant. 'Let's wait a moment.'

George stopped in surprise, holding her penknife.

'What do you mean?' she whispered. 'Don't you want me to set you free?'

'No – I have a better idea,' Mrs Grant whispered back. 'You say your cousin has gone for the police? Well, those men came here to steal my emeralds, and if they get hold of them, they'll make off straight away. I'd like to save my jewels – and I'd very much like to see the thieves arrested too. So they mustn't suspect that you're here. You must take the emeralds and get them safely out of the house. They'll go on searching the place, and when they don't find anything they'll come back here to question me and search this room, too. All of that will take some time. I hope I can keep them here, talking, until police reinforcements arrive. The only thing is – it's rather dangerous. I'm not sure whether I ought to tell you where I've hidden the jewels.'

'In case I rob you?' asked George, with a rather wry smile.

'In case they catch you!' replied Mrs Grant, sighing.

George was quick to reassure her.

'Don't worry,' she said. 'I shall keep very, very quiet. I'll do exactly as you say – so just trust me.'

Mrs Grant was still hesitating. She didn't want

George to run any unnecessary risks. But George was impatient.

'We're terribly short of time,' she said. 'If we're to act, we must do it quickly. I suppose your jewel case *isn't* in your bedroom? I can hear Karl and Co. searching up there.'

Mrs Grant suddenly made up her mind.

'You're right,' she said. 'While they're busy elsewhere, you'll have time to get the emeralds and take them away. No, the jewel case isn't in my bedroom. It's hidden on one of the big beams in the attic – the beam on your left as you go in. You'll find it easily enough. The staircase up to the attic is rather a steep one, and you'll see it at the end of the corridor, by the kitchen door. Hurry up, my dear, and try not to let them catch you. If any harm came to you I should never forgive myself!' She added, with a smile, 'And when the thieves find me still tied to this chair, they won't have the faintest idea that I've outwitted them. Off you go, then, and do be quick!'

George left the room. But before making for the end of the corridor she ran on tiptoe to the front door and opened it. She didn't even need to call Timmy! Her faithful dog was always ready to obey her. He followed George without a sound. Both of them started to climb the attic stairs, keeping very quiet.

It was not an easy climb. The wooden stairs tended to creak under George's weight, light as she was. But at last she and Tim reached the top. George pushed open the door, which gave way with a slight groan of its hinges. She listened carefully, but the thieves were still searching the first floor.

George switched on the light and looked round. The attic contained trunks, boxes, and piles of cardboard cartons. Everything was very neat and tidy. Big, solid wooden beams ran under the tiled roof. Following Mrs Grant's instructions, George found a small stool in a corner, and placed it to the left of the doorway. Then she climbed up on the stool. Timmy was watching all her movements closely.

Slowly, George ran her hand along the top of the big beam. Suddenly she uttered a squeal of joy, which she just as quickly stifled.

'We've done it, Tim! I've got it!'

She jumped down from her perch, feeling very excited, and holding the pretty, inlaid box she had just found.

She opened it with a hand that trembled slightly – and took out the most magnificent piece of jewellery! It blazed with a thousand little flames of green fire in the faint light of the electric bulb hanging from the attic ceiling. It was a superb emerald necklace! No doubt Mrs Grant's ancestor had had Queen Victoria's emeralds set like this in order to give them to a member of his family as a present – perhaps his wife or sweet-heart.

'Isn't it beautiful?' whispered George admiringly. 'Did you ever see anything so lovely, Tim? Well, come on, old fellow – let's hurry off and put the jewels somewhere safe.'

At that very moment she heard the thieves climbing the stairs to the attic!

Standing there by the doorway, George was panic-stricken for a moment. Yes, she was quite right – men's heavy footsteps were certainly clumping up the wooden stairs to the attic.

The criminals must have heard her, and were coming to see what was going on.

His coat bristling, Timmy began to growl at the door. George looked round, searching for some other way of escape from the attic. But she could not see any way out except for a small skylight above her head, too high up for her to reach it even if she stood on the stool. And anyway, there wasn't time. What was she going to do?

Chapter Fifteen

WHERE ARE THE EMERALDS?

The thieves climbed up the stairs to the attic without bothering to take any precautions.

'I tell you, I did hear a noise up there,' Dave was saying. 'I have very good hearing. Look! There's a light on in the attic.'

'Hm!' grunted Lenny. 'So Mrs Grant wasn't alone in the house after all!'

'Let me past,' said Karl.

He was the first to enter the attic. Just at that moment, a huge dog almost knocked him off his feet as it shot past, making its way between his legs. Karl swore out loud, and then roared with laughter. 'Come on, you two!' he cried. 'It's nothing to worry about! Only a little girl, up here on her own!'

'I know her!' cried Dave, coming into the attic. 'She's one of the children from Kirrin village. But what's she doing here?'

'Perhaps she's a relation of Mrs Grant's?' suggested Lenny.

Then Karl suddenly saw the stool underneath the beam. His face brightened.

'Never mind that!' he said. 'If you ask me, this little girl was after the emeralds herself. And she was cleverer than us, too – she found them first! Look at that jewel case on the floor!'

The scene spoke for itself. The criminals could see what had happened. There was George, kneeling on the dusty floor of the attic, with the closed jewel case in front of her beside the stool, which was still in place below the beam.

'You found the case up on that beam, did you, eh?' said Karl. 'Right – hand it over, now!'

George snatched up the jewel case and clutched it to her chest. 'You shan't have it!' she said defiantly.

'We'll see about that, little girl! Your dog didn't even stay to defend you, did he? *He* ran away when he scented danger. And we can be very dangerous when people get in our way – so hand it over!'

Karl came forward, and, in spite of George's resistance, he grabbed the jewel case and got it away from her. Then he opened it. Lenny and Dave craned forward to have a look.

The jewel case was empty!

Karl looked at George, his eyes blazing.

'Where are the emeralds?' he asked in a voice

like thunder. 'Give them to me, or you'll be sorry!'

'Emeralds? What emeralds?' George sounded puzzled.

'Don't you try fooling us, or you'll be sorry! Go on, you two, search the whole place. She can't have hidden the jewels very far away.'

While Dave made George turn her pockets out, Karl and Lenny started a thorough search of the attic. They pushed over all the piles of cardboard cartons and looked inside all the trunks. They searched every nook and cranny. All in vain! They did not find anything!

Then Karl came back to George, looking very threatening.

'Where are those emeralds?' he repeated. There was a dangerous gleam in his eye.

'The case was empty when I found it,' said George sulkily.

'That's what *you* say! I've had enough of this. You're coming downstairs with us, and Mrs Grant will tell us where to find them soon enough.'

Holding George by the arm, Karl made her climb down the attic stairs. On the ground floor, Mrs Grant had heard cries and the sound of footsteps, so she was not very surprised when she saw George appear with Dave and Lenny one on each side of her, though she did turn rather pale. She was horrified to think of what had happened.

Karl came into the room, beside himself with anger.

'This child found a jewel case in the attic,' he said, 'but there's no sign of the emeralds inside it.'

If that gave Mrs Grant a shock, she hid it carefully. She had made up her mind to protect George as well as she possibly could, and she cleverly invented an explanation on the spot.

'Of course not!' she said, with a mocking laugh. 'This child is one of your gang! She asked me to tell her where the treasure was hidden, but I sent her off on a false trail. It's no good expecting *me* to tell you where the jewels are!'

'This little girl has nothing to do with us!' said Lenny angrily. 'But we have a good idea she was trying to steal the emeralds for herself! So she didn't find anything either!'

'We know that!' said Dave. 'We found her kneeling in the attic beside the empty jewel case. She can't possibly have had time to hide the emeralds anywhere!'

As Karl himself was convinced that George was only another thief, though rather a young one, he took no more notice of her, and turned his attention to Mrs Grant.

'Now, you listen to me!' he cried. 'You may have been able to deceive this girl – she's still very young – but you can't pull the wool over *our* eyes! You're going to tell us where those emeralds are hidden, here and now, and if you don't, we shall lock you in your cellar and leave you there without food or water until you give in!'

Mrs Grant glanced surreptitiously at the clock on the mantelpiece. Whatever happened, she had to hold out until the reinforcements George had promised came. And there was only one way to do that – she must keep the thieves occupied searching for the treasure as long as necessary, to give the police and Dick time to arrive.

So she pretended to be giving in after all.

'Oh, very well,' she sighed, in an exhausted voice. 'You win! But you'll find it isn't easy to get your hands on the emeralds. That jewel case in the attic was only there to mislead any burglars. In fact, I took the emeralds out of their case and sealed them up in a hiding place inside the chimney leading from the fireplace in my bedroom. Whichever of you is the thinnest,' Mrs Grant went on, 'will have to wriggle up the chimney pipe and use a hammer and chisel to get one of the bricks out. It's a brick in the nineteenth row up from floor level – and the fourth one on the left. You'll find tools in the boot of my car out in the garage.'

Lenny and Dave were already making for the door when Karl called them back.

'Just a moment – tie the little girl up too! I don't want her making off before we've got hold of the jewels and left the country. We'll leave her here with Mrs Grant. The police will set them free later, when we're safely away. I may even phone them myself just before we leave – ha, ha, ha!'

He went on laughing, rubbing his hands with glee, while Lenny and Dave tied George to a chair opposite Mrs Grant. Then the three thieves went off to go out to the garage and find the bag of tools. As soon as the sound of their footsteps had died away, Mrs Grant whispered, 'The emeralds! What did you do with them?'

'Don't worry,' George told her. 'They're in a safe place. But what about you? You told the thieves where to find the jewels, and they'll be angry when they don't find anything there!'

'I'm hoping that their search will keep them busy till the police arrive.'

'So long as they don't realise you were playing a trick on them before help comes – ssh! They're on their way back.'

Chapter Sixteen

ALL ENDS WELL

However, the thieves did not come into the room where their two prisoners were sitting. They couldn't wait to get at the chimney where the treasure was hidden!

Motionless, Mrs Grant and George listened to the three of them hammering away at the chimney-piece overhead. Mrs Grant smiled.

'It's very solidly built,' she said, 'and that noise they're making will drown the sound of the police arriving. Oh dear, how slowly the minutes seem to be passing.'

George had no time to reply – she had just caught the sound of someone moving quietly about in the garden.

'There's someone coming,' she thought. 'Oh, if only it could be Dick!' And it really was Dick! He had guided the police cautiously along the gravel path to the front door of Manners House.

Julian and Anne insisted on bringing up the rear. The sergeant found the front door itself open, and signalled to his men.

'Follow me!' he said quietly. 'You children wait outside!'

The police entered the sitting room on the ground floor, and stared at the sight of the two prisoners tied to their chairs. 'Quick!' said Mrs Grant. 'You can set us free later. Get hold of those men first! Can you hear them? They're up in my bedroom on the first floor.'

The sergeant was a man of action. Followed by other police officers, he dashed upstairs, and flung open the bedroom door.

'Got you!' he cried.

Seeing the police appear so suddenly, Karl and Lenny were rooted to the ground with surprise. Handcuffs clicked shut around their wrists as they were cautioned. They were under arrest! As for Dave, who was halfway up the chimney, the police got him out black with soot, and obviously completely baffled.

Outside, Julian, Dick and Anne were getting impatient, and they decided not to wait for the police to come back.

'George is somewhere in there – I'm sure she is,' said Dick. 'Otherwise we'd have seen her by now! Let's go and help her!'

The boys hurried into the house, followed by Anne, who was too worried about her cousin to feel frightened. The children saw George and Mrs Grant at once, and Julian and Dick quickly set them free, cutting the ropes which bound them with their penknives.

'Oh, my dear children!' said Mrs Grant, deeply touched. 'I can never thank you enough! And to think I was so suspicious of you the first time you came to this house!'

Anne looked round.

'Where's Timmy?' she asked George. 'Didn't he stay to protect you? Or have those awful men hurt him?'

But George did not have time to open her mouth and reply. The policemen were coming back already, with the handcuffed figures of Karl, Lenny and Dave.

'Here are our men – caught in the act!' said the sergeant cheerfully. 'Good work, that! You have these young people to thank for it, ma'am. It's all due to them that we were able to catch this little lot!'

The criminals looked at George. Plainly, they were puzzled. They were amazed to see her free, and apparently on good terms with Mrs Grant. The girl saw what they were thinking. 'No, I'm *not* a thief!' she told them, laughing. 'In fact, just the opposite, as you can see – because, along with my cousins here, *I'm* responsible for getting you arrested!'

Lenny, still furious at having failed, said

venomously, 'And what *did* you do with the emeralds?'

'She can't possibly have them!' said Karl resentfully. 'We searched everywhere.'

'So you did,' agreed the sergeant. 'Miss Kirrin, do you know where Mrs Grant's jewels are?'

George gave a mischievous smile, and did not reply straight away. Mrs Grant, Julian, Dick, Anne, the thieves and the police were all watching her. They seemed to be hanging on her words.

'Karl is right,' she said at last. 'I haven't got Mrs Grant's emeralds!'

'But – ' stammered Mrs Grant, taken aback. 'But you said – '

'They aren't even in the house,' George went on, taking no notice of the interruption.

Everyone began to talk at once, firing off questions, but no one answered them. George started to laugh, and raised her hand for silence. Then, turning to Mrs Grant, she said, 'I'm telling the truth when I say the emeralds aren't here – but no one has stolen them, and I promise you they're in a safe place!'

Julian, Dick and Anne were intrigued, but they knew their cousin well enough to trust her! So they waited in silence to hear the rest of the story.

'The emeralds are at Kirrin,' George went on. 'And if Mrs Grant wouldn't mind driving us there in her car, I can give her back her property!'

A moment later, a strange procession set off

through the dark, making for Kirrin. The policemen and their prisoners piled into the police car. Mrs Grant, who had quickly put on some outdoor clothes, followed them at the wheel of her own car. She had the children with her, but she did not ask them any questions. By now she trusted George completely.

Before they set off, George had asked the police sergeant if he would stop at Kirrin Cottage. So they all stopped outside Aunt Fanny and Uncle Quentin's house, and the sergeant left his men guarding the thieves while, torch in hand, he followed George. She guided her companions to – Timmy's kennel!

'Timmy!' she called. 'Good dog, Tim!'

The dog came out of his kennel, jumping for joy, and put his forepaws up on George's shoulders. Then Mrs Grant, Julian, Dick and Anne uttered a cry of amazement. The police sergeant looked very surprised too! Because, round his neck, Timmy was wearing the most magnificent emerald necklace any of them had ever seen!

'Your jewels!' said George, taking them off Timmy to hand them back to their owner. 'You see, when I heard the men coming up to the attic I realised I simply didn't have time to hide the necklace anywhere. So I put it round Timmy's neck and told him to run to Kirrin Cottage as fast as he could go. "Kennel!" I told him – and he always obeys me, you see. I hope, just for once,

Father won't say I've been over-imaginative!'

After that, everyone was full of praise and congratulations for the Five. But as for the children themselves, there was only one thing they badly wanted to do that night – get back to Kirrin Island for some well-earned sleep!

Another new adventure of the
characters created by Enid Blyton,
told by Claude Voilier and translated
by Anthea Bell:

THE FAMOUS FIVE AND THE
STATELY HOMES GANG

The Five are pleased to be spending
another holiday at Kirrin Cottage, the
scene of many of their adventures.
And this holiday proves to be as
exciting as all the others from the
moment they set off on their shiny
new bicycles!

Also available . . .

THE FAMOUS FIVE AND THE
    MISSING CHEETAH
THE FAMOUS FIVE GO ON
    TELEVISION
THE FAMOUS FIVE VERSUS
    THE BLACK MASK
THE FAMOUS FIVE AND THE
    GOLDEN GALLEON
THE FAMOUS FIVE IN FANCY DRESS
THE FAMOUS FIVE AND THE
    BLUE BEAR MYSTERY

KNIGHT BOOKS